I0533915

BREAKFAST ON BELGRAVIA

By Darci Leigh

Cover Photo

By

Dennis Paul

ACKNOWLEDGEMENTS

To my husband, Dennis, who encouraged and supported me, literally for years, as I gave birth to this *baby*. His heart is as much a part of this accomplishment as is mine.

To my intelligent, gorgeous, and fabulous daughters, Michelle and Emily, who are my constant cheerleaders.

To my six grandchildren, three from each daughter, whose collective light illumines my path.

To Janice D. Faulkner Cowen, aka Aunt Jan, whose unconditional love and encouragement kept me on track.

To my dear friends, Barb and her late husband Lou, who introduced me to the historical St. James Court in Louisville, Kentucky and who were host and hostess supreme of many gatherings of which I was fortunate to be a part. I dedicate this novel to them.

I am blessed.

Chapter 1

Lillie locked the closet door, turned around and rested her back against it as she caught her breath. *How much longer*, she wondered to herself as she closed her eyes for a moment to decompress. She swept her hair off her face, straightened her apron, and slipped out of 3-B, locking the door behind her, without being seen. She tiptoed quietly down the stairs and returned to her quarters to clean herself up before starting breakfast.

A breeze drifted into 2-A through a small opening in the window, and the subtle sunlight made it known that a new day had arrived. As the morning called to her, Amy opened her eyes to see her beloved lying next to her. She placed her arm around his warm body, pulled herself in closer, and cherished the moment. She closed her eyes again and got goosebumps as she recalled making love with Drew the night before.

Dr. Vic in 2-B chose that room specifically for its darkness. When he came to *The Lillie Inn Bed and Breakfast*, it was usually the only time he could sleep in, and the last thing he wanted to see early on a Saturday was light making its way into the room and interrupting his much-needed and longed-for rest. It would be noon before his eyes would welcome visions of anything that wasn't in his dreams.

The bed was meticulously made, and the drapes were pulled as though they had not been drawn at all the night before. If not for the fluffy purple slippers parked neatly under the nightstand, one might easily assume there was no guest occupying 2-C. Waking up was Joan's favorite time of every day, especially when visiting the bed and breakfast. It was not necessary to wait for the sun to get up. There was always a book to read or something to journal or time to reserve for a quiet meditation. With her vibrant personality, this attractive woman in her mid-sixties was already on her morning stroll. Soon she would come walking into the foyer, ready to enjoy breakfast and meet her fellow guests. Her regular visits were anxiously anticipated by Lillie, the innkeeper, who was busy brewing Joan's favorite decaf tea.

Up the wooden staircase to the third floor were two more rooms, 3-A and 3-C. Unlike the en suites on the second floor, the rooms on the third floor shared one bath. Those rooms were less expensive but equally treasured by their guests. That weekend, 3-A was occupied by a young woman about whom little was known. Maddie learned about the inn online, and it was the first time she had stayed there. She arrived mid-afternoon on the Friday before, and once she was in her room, no one had seen her.

Michael in 3-C had been a registered guest since Wednesday. A journalist for a travel magazine, Michael was writing a story on a unique Louisville restaurant called *Lynn's* where he had eaten lunch on Wednesday, dinner on Thursday, and breakfast on Friday. Today he would enjoy breakfast at the inn with the others.

The smallest of all the accommodations, 3-B was not registered to anyone.

Lillie was proud of her bed and breakfast. She had acquired it with an inheritance received from her maternal grandparents who passed away years ago, when she was too young to remember. A trust had been established for Lillie from which she was able to withdraw when she turned twenty-five. Until then, she had no idea of its existence, as her parents agreed that her awareness of the trust might cause her to make some hasty decisions. Lillie believed her parents thought wisely, and she was proud of her thoughtful investment.

Joan paced herself so she could enjoy every step of her stroll. She appreciated the birds chirping and the leaves scattering in the breeze. Sounds of distant traffic reminded her of how fortunate she was to have the opportunity to get away from the busyness of the world and relish in some simple pleasures.

As she approached the inn, Joan stopped and admired the architecture of the well-built structure. Three stories high and made of red brick, this century-old residence was said to have been host to Thomas Edison when he visited the town he called home over a hundred years ago. The long front porch had been host to many friendly gatherings over the years, and it beckoned those who walked by. Rich, deep-green ivy had been climbing the structure for years, and it followed a well-thought-out path, working its way up the walls and around doors and windows as if it knew not to block the view.

Belgravia Court had become well-known for the dozens of cats that believed this neighborhood was their residence, and the inn shared in the responsibility of caring for them. Residents could not stroll down Belgravia Court without a cat or two crossing their path. The houses along Belgravia and the famous St. James Court were built close together. Louisville, Kentucky, is acclaimed for its kind hospitality, and locals appreciate living in close proximity to one another. They make it a point to become familiar with their neighbors; there are no strangers here.

The smell of cooked bacon greeted Joan as she stepped onto the porch and entered the foyer. The new springs on the screen door made certain it was tightly closed. She followed the aroma into the dining room where Lillie had just placed a generous platter of bacon next to an assortment of other delectable offerings on the table.

Joan began salivating as she gazed across the spread of orange-cranberry nut muffins, poached eggs, blueberry pancakes with hot maple syrup, and homemade breads with a variety of jams and jellies. It was always a challenge for Joan to contain her joy—and why should she? With utter delight, she began to giggle at this most inviting feast. She could hardly wait for the others to hurry down and join her for their first meal together, and she took her place at the table, fulfilling her hope to be the first person present. She waited in anticipation of who might take the seat next to her. She didn't have to wait long. By the sound of the slippers shuffling across the wooden floor, Joan knew expect at least two people.

"Good morning," Amy greeted in a soft voice. Her hair was pulled back in a ponytail, and she wore a beautiful pink cotton robe with matching slippers. She walked arm in arm with Drew, her husband of eight years, who looked half-asleep. They both seemed so young.

"Good morning!" Joan replied with a little more enthusiasm than Drew could understand for so early on a Saturday. Nonetheless, he responded politely with a simple and quiet "morning" as he pulled out a chair for his wife. Amy took her seat while glancing up toward her handsome husband as if to say thank you. Drew sat next to her and they placed napkins on their laps while they gazed over the tempting display of food.

"Isn't it lovely? I don't know where to begin!" Joan exclaimed.

Lillie entered the dining room to find two new guests were seated, and she poured them each a cup of freshly brewed coffee. "Hazelnut cream today," she announced.

"May I have decaf, please?" Amy asked, and Lillie obliged.

Joan helped herself to one of the muffins, placed a pad of butter on the top and watched it melt as she stirred her tea. She positioned her spoon on her saucer and offered her hand to Amy and then Drew.

"Joan Jennings," she blurted out. "It's my pleasure."

Amy accepted her offer and found Ms. Jennings to have a solid handshake.

"Amy—Amy Stout, and this is my husband, Drew," who extended his hand.

"Forgive me, Ms. Jennings, but we didn't get much sleep last night." Amy batted her eyes as she looked down, so Joan wouldn't notice her blush. Joan smiled.

A door opened on the third floor, then closed quickly. Footsteps could be heard making their way to the staircase before descending the first flight of steps, then the second. Michael paused in the foyer and breathed in deeply the aroma before he turned toward the dining room. The sun at his back silhouetted his strapping physique, and he was an image to behold. Those already seated couldn't help but notice him as he turned toward them and observed the magnificent feast. A smile came across his face that could have easily melted the butter sitting on the table. Food…this man loved food…after all, it was how he made his living. Michael took his seat at the head of the table, where he clearly belonged.

Michael was a ruggedly handsome man of solid stature. He was six feet and four inches of muscle, which he had developed playing sports in high school and college. Now in his late-thirties with a head of thick, deep brown hair, he commanded attention without effort when entering a room, and this morning was no exception. He had a big personality that complemented his build, and he was not one to be ignored.

"Good morning!" he bellowed. "Michael Roth here." He grabbed his napkin, tossed it on his lap and exclaimed, "Lillie, the next time I come here, I am writing an article about you and your magnificent meals!"

Lillie smiled with pride as she entered the room with the pot of hot coffee. "I would like that," she said, as she reached around his neck and gave him a big hug. Michael had been here before, many times, and over the years Lillie had developed a fondness for him…like that of a big brother she never had.

"Joan Jennings," she announced once again as she reached out her hand to Michael.

"The pleasure is mine," he stated. Then he looked toward Amy and Drew, who picked up their cue and introduced themselves.

"I don't mean to be rude, but I hope we're not waiting for everyone to arrive before we dig in." Michael picked up the plate of bacon and helped himself before passing it to Joan.

Everyone immediately joined in, and all that could be heard was the clanking of utensils followed by sounds of contentment as they all sampled the array of breakfast treats. Dr. Vic was sleeping through this marvelous meal; he never knew what he missed.

With everyone so involved in the eating frenzy, no one noticed the swoosh of black sweats that rushed through the foyer until after the screen door slammed shut. Lillie had just finished pouring a second cup of coffee for Drew when her attention was diverted by the loud noise. She turned her head toward the front window to see her young guest from 3-A begin her morning jog down Belgravia Court and onto St. James Court toward Central Park.

"Oh my," exclaimed Lillie, "I almost forgot about Maddie. I guess she isn't hungry this morning."

"Maddie?" Michael inquired.

"Your housemate in 3-A. I don't know much about her, but she seems very nice. She's a new guest from West Virginia. I look forward to getting to know her—though it may be difficult. She keeps to herself." Lillie finished filling coffee cups and walked toward the kitchen.

Michael wiped his mouth with the linen napkin and placed it next to his plate. He took a deep breath, patted his satisfied belly, and thanked Lillie for one of the best meals he had consumed in a long time. She blushed as she revealed a modest smile and wondered how many times he had used that line.

Michael excused himself, bidding everyone a pleasant day. Drew and Amy sipped the last of their coffee and juice and together made their way back up to their room. Joan had not even noticed that no one sat next to her. She stood up and started clearing the table when Lillie insisted she go and enjoy her day.

"As insane as it sounds, I actually enjoy cleaning the table and the dishes; that way I notice what everyone liked eating, or what they didn't. It helps me with my meal planning. Anyway, you are here to relax, and it is a beautiful day."

Joan thanked Lillie and retired to the front porch.

Chapter 2

Joan perched herself on a rocking chair and enjoyed the crisp air of the lovely fall morning. She leaned her head back, and before she knew it, her eyes closed, and she was fast asleep. An hour passed before Joan woke up. She looked at her watch and couldn't believe it. She stretched her arms and took a deep breath that turned into a yawn. Joan appreciated how easy it was for her to relax here. As she gazed around the porch, she quickly realized she wasn't alone. Michael was occupying another rocking chair.

"Oh my! How long have you been out here?"

"Only a few minutes," he replied. "I have almost completed my article, but I didn't want to miss this perfect morning, and I didn't have the heart to wake you."

Just then, Maddie returned from her jog. Her black running gear was drenched in sweat, and much of her long dark hair had made its way out of its ponytail. She stopped on the porch to catch her breath; her face was flushed and her brow dripping with perspiration. She dabbed her forehead with her left wristband while she supported herself, bent over, with her right arm.

"Are you alright?" Joan asked.

Without even looking up, Maddie nodded, still trying to catch her breath.

"How about some water?" Michael asked.

Again, without eye contact, Maddie nodded and managed a thumbs-up sign.

Michael returned within a minute, and Maddie drank the entire glass without stopping before it was empty.

"Looks like you need to sit for a while, young lady," remarked the always-maternal Joan, and Maddie must have thought it was a good idea, as she dropped her tired body into a third rocking chair. It didn't take long before she was breathing at a regular pace, and normal color returned to her face.

"That was quite a workout," Michael said. "You've been running for over an hour."

"I love to run," Maddie remarked. "It's excellent therapy. Central Park was summoning me," she said with a chuckle. "They're setting up a stage for a performance tonight...pretty cool, I think. The actors were rehearsing as I was running, and people were walking their dogs. This city likes to wake up early and get going. I really love it here in the fall."

"Better than West Virginia?" Michael asked.

Maddie quickly turned her head toward him. "Have we met?"

"Oh—no, but Lillie told us you were from West Virginia as you jogged out the door this morning."

"Oh," she said apologetically. "Yes—better than West Virginia."

Michael sensed he hit a sore spot. "Well, you inspire me. The way I eat, I certainly should at least consider such vigorous exercise. And I'm not getting any younger!"

Maddie smiled. "Well, thanks for the water—I really need to get in the shower."

As she walked through the doorway, Michael couldn't help but notice how well running had served Maddie. Her muscle tone gave her the appearance of a true athlete, and he went out of his way to watch her as she disappeared up the stairs. The expression on his face let Joan know that he was impressed with this attractive young woman.

"So, Michael, what's your story?" Joan asked, but there was no answer. He appeared lost in thought.

A little louder this time, Joan asked, "So, Michael, tell me about yourself."

Hearing his name mentioned, Michael cleared his throat and started stuttering, "Uh, em…um—excuse me?" he responded.

"Tell me about yourself," Joan inquired again.

"Oh, I'm sorry—I was preoccupied for a moment there," Michael said.

"Yes, I noticed."

"Well," Michael began, "not an interesting story, really. You know I am a writer for a travel magazine, right?" Joan nodded. "It's a great job—getting paid to travel and write about it. I have been all over the world. I have stayed at the most impressive hotels and eaten at restaurants intended to serve only the elite. I have met many fine folks in my travels, and life is good."

Michael paused for a moment and became more comfortable in his rocking chair. He pulled another chair closer with his right leg and threw his left leg onto the seat, then crossed it with the right. He rested his head onto the back of the chair and gazed out toward the court. The breeze was calm, and although it was late September, the leaves were already starting to gather on the ground from the surrounding trees. "My life has been a busy one, though," he hesitated, "and a fulfilling one," and he hesitated again.

Joan was an intuitive person, and she knew how to be a good listener. She followed her instincts, sitting quietly and patiently during Michael's pauses, as she could see he was giving serious thought to her question.

"I've never been married," he continued. "Been with lots of women," and he paused as if he were recalling some of his experiences, then he reiterated and emphasized "lots…and lots, but I never settled down. Not because I didn't think about it; I gave it serious thought at one point." Michael's mind wandered and Joan began to wonder why she thought this was any of her business at all. She didn't mean to pry; her interest was genuine, and not just about Michael but in everyone she met.

Michael continued, "But you know—I just don't think I'm the settling-down type. I don't have any children—at least not that I know of," and he chuckled at himself until he realized that line isn't funny anymore. "Well, hell, you know, my life story just isn't that interesting," he repeated and he hem-hawed and stuttered as he searched his memory in an effort to identify something spectacular to report.

"I have had many great opportunities, met hundreds of fun and colorful people, but whatever that one thing is that would make my life really interesting…well, I just haven't had that experience yet." Michael had that look on his face that one gets when looking back in review.

"I can't change the past, and I don't think I want to; it's been awesome! Most people would likely think I have had an interesting life, but something needs to change…I'm ready for something different, a new focus…something more satisfying." He paused.

"Yes…satisfying seems the right word. Well, as I said earlier, I'm not getting any younger, and boy, don't I know it. I might even have trouble getting out of this rocking chair." He looked at Joan, sitting contently, listening and nodding her head. Michael admired how sincere she seemed.

Joan was an attractive, mature lady in her mid-sixties. Her beautiful silver hair had traces of black peppered throughout. Her short, no-hassle hairstyle suited her well, and hanging around her neck was a pair of reading glasses on a long-beaded chain. She was wearing a casual running suit, however, the intention of running in it had never occurred to her, and Michael would notice by Sunday afternoon that the shoes she was wearing were one of several pairs she had in different colors. Michael was comfortable with this woman whom he didn't know, and if he were going to share his story with anyone, she would be the one. But instead, Michael asked,

"So, Joan, won't you tell me about yourself? What brings you to this town of Old Louisville, and more specifically, this bed and breakfast?"

"Oh, I had friends on St. James Court years ago, and I enjoy coming back, especially in the fall when the leaves are turning, and the climate is still comfortable—you know, before it gets too cold." She paused. "I despise the cold." She shook her shoulders as she shuddered at the thought of winter right around the corner.

"My friends were a lovely couple who, like so many in Old Louisville, didn't just buy their home—they adopted it and made it their own. They updated the entire structure while preserving its unique history, and then they filled the home with love and new life. They decorated in showcase style—down to the final detail. The kitchen was enlarged to allow a sizable gathering, and because everyone enjoyed congregating in that room, they separated the kitchen from the back deck by a wall of windows and glass doors that when opened extended into one enormous room with lovely, well-manicured gardens. It was delightful, to say the least. They were friends to so many and entertained often. I was one of their fortunate and frequent guests. Sadly, though, the husband died unexpectedly a couple of years ago, and his wife was devastated—we were all devastated." Joan sighed and continued with *her story*.

"Unlike you, Michael, I have been married—twice, in fact!" and she laughed at herself. "You know, not many women my age are quick to acknowledge multiple marriages. Back in my day, women were supposed to get married and stay married. Many folks were not understanding of the *Big D*—you know, divorce. But, hey, I've never been a conformist. I loved both of my husbands very much, and I had two children with my first husband and was a good stepmother to my second husband's two children, all grown now. Maybe I'm not the settling-down type, either.

"Oh, well, apparently unlike you, my life has been interesting—and fun, and it has also been difficult and sad and sometimes painful. But it has been rich, and when I look back, I don't feel sorry for myself. I am grateful for both the good and the not-so-good times, and the not-so-good times made me stronger and wiser. Anyway, it is what it is, and the past is behind me. For now, I enjoy moments like this, meeting people like you and sitting aimlessly on a porch, watching leaves fall from trees and listening to birds sing and smelling apple pie cooking in the oven and—oh my, apple pie! I love apple pie, don't you?! Can you smell it, too?"

Michael sat up in his chair and started sniffing, his nose bobbing around in midair as if he were trying to catch the aroma. "I have a professional smelling nose, you know, and I believe you are correct." Like schoolchildren, the two leaped out of their chairs and raced into the kitchen.

Lillie had just taken three apple pies out of the oven and placed them on the windowsill, and in the cool, autumn mid-morning, it was easy to see heat rising as steam filled the air.

"Now this," Michael stated, "is a moment worth remembering." He reached forward to catch some of the filling running over the edge of the pie shell.

Lillie caught his hand and began scolding him. "At least wait until it cools, Mr. Roth."

Michael couldn't remember the last time he was scolded or the last time he was referred to as Mr. Roth. While Lillie still had a hold of his hand, he turned it palm side up and gently held her hand in his. He drew her silken hand to his mouth and kissed it in gratitude.

"Lillie, you are remarkable," he bellowed, and once again, Lillie blushed. She stood there for a moment, looking into Michael's eyes, as if no one, not even Michael, noticed. Suddenly, she realized that he was still holding her hand, and in her embarrassment, she quickly pulled it away and wrapped it in a towel that was hanging conveniently on her apron.

She cleared her throat and announced that dinner would be served at 6 o'clock. "And if you eat all your dinner, you will get your pie…ala mode, if you prefer." Joan and Michael both laughed and promised to be on time.

"Good," Lillie responded with a smile. "You know the only time I prepare dinner is when you are here, Michael."

"Oh, yes—I know, and I'm looking forward to it."

Chapter 3

Lillie was a delightful little girl growing up, with big blue eyes and curly, chestnut-brown hair that she usually wore pulled back in a ponytail. Her mother loved and adored her little Lillie, and she wanted her to know how lovable she was. Lillie was sweet and had good manners; she never caused a moment of stress for anyone, which was important to her mother because she knew Lillie's good behavior was the only way she could protect herself from her father's cruelty.

Lillie was not aware of her father's abusive behavior for years during which time she and her mother developed a very close relationship. Her mother protected her as long as she could, but eventually Lillie learned of her father's mistreatment, and because of this nasty family secret, Lillie rarely had friends over; in fact, she had very few friends. Being social was never simple for her since she was embarrassed by her family situation, and avoiding a social life was easier than explaining the truth. She learned to keep her relationships at a distance.

Lillie barely made it through high school (not because she wasn't smart; she was definitely smart, but there were days she simply couldn't go because of the bruises on her legs, arms and back). Her wicked father was very careful to never strike her in the face, but the nights of endless crying caused her face to swell so much that she didn't dare go to school. Her beatings became more frequent as she grew older, and she didn't know where to turn. Her mother was not very helpful, as she, too, was a victim of this miserable man's unwillingness to control his anger.

The manipulation took its toll on her emotions—as well as her mother's. When her father could not abuse them physically, he would torment them with condescending and painful remarks. He was a hateful man, and Lillie could never figure out why her mother married him in the first place.

Following some of the insane tirades, Lillie's mother would try to help Lillie understand that her father didn't really intend any harm. She said he learned this behavior growing up, and he knew no other way to express his disappointment or anger. She tried to help Lillie realize that these episodes had nothing to do with her—that they were completely her father's responsibility and issues. She asked Lillie to think of the good times, yet Lillie believed he was nothing but evil. Out of respect for her mother, Lillie tried to hold her tongue and exercise good behavior, but deep down she loathed this man, and she despised those who had taught him to be so evil. She often thought to herself that her life would never be good until that hateful man was dead and gone, and though she was ashamed and confused by those thoughts and feelings, she wished him dead every day.

Lillie could remember cooking with her mother from a very young age—so young that she couldn't reach the kitchen counter. She would pull up a chair to stand on while she helped make bread and bake pies. Lillie didn't know it at the time, but cooking and baking were her mother's attempts to keep her husband as happy and quiet as possible. At first, this worked for her all the time, but even the best apple pie wasn't enough to soften this angry man's heart. Lillie watched her mother endure beatings by her father, and as she grew older, she would try to defend her mother, but all that did was make her father even angrier. She remembered wanting to learn how to cook breads and pies to please her father, hoping he would stop beating them both. Now, all these years later, Lillie continued making breads, pies and other fine foods, and still for the pleasure of others, only now it was far more rewarding.

Lillie was an efficient innkeeper who completed most of her tasks in the mornings. Afternoons she saved for herself. Once the pies were safe from hungry eyes, she retreated to her suite in the back of the inn near the kitchen—originally the maid's quarters. It served Lillie very well. When she needed to get breakfast started early, she never had to be concerned that her guests would be disturbed by the noise she made as she prepared their meals. Although Lillie never prepared them, lunch items were always available and guests could help themselves, which is how she ran into Dr. Vic that beautiful Saturday afternoon.

Lillie had just finished her bubble bath, a regular Saturday ritual. She applied lavender lotion and after-bath talc onto her small, slender frame before she slipped into a long cotton smock and a pair of mules. She threw a sweater over her shoulders and walked into the kitchen. There he was, Dr. Vic, standing in front of the refrigerator, door wide open, and studying its contents as if he were gathering information for a research project. He was so absorbed in his efforts to find something that appealed to his appetite, he didn't even notice Lillie walking into the room. "Well, hello, Dr. Vic. It's good to see you!"

Dr. Vic quickly turned around to see Lillie standing there, as sweet as the last time he saw her. Her long dark hair was pulled up off her neck and held in place by an elastic scrunchy. Her pale skin highlighted her blue eyes, and she was the only woman Dr. Vic knew who enjoyed wearing no makeup. "Lillie, you are a sight for sore eyes," he said, as he reached out to greet her with a warm hug.

"You must be starving" she responded, as she started to run down a list of food options. She called off the leftovers from breakfast, added some chicken salad made fresh the day before, and finished with an offer of apple pie if he promised not to tell the others.

Dr. Vic's eyes lit up at the thought of apple pie, and he accepted her offer. "With ice cream?" he asked, and Lillie obliged. She brewed him a fresh cup of coffee and served him his pie in the kitchen. "Sit down with me, Lillie, and bring me up to date with yourself. What's new?"

Lillie was flattered that he wanted her to sit with him. She poured herself a cup of coffee and had a seat. "Not much is new," she reported. "Mama has been gone five years now, and I still miss her, but I love this place, and I love the people I meet every week. I love cooking for them, watching them eat and enjoy the food. I like to tell them about the city, and the best places to visit. It's both the same and yet different. I really enjoy it. What's new with you since your last visit?"

"Same-old, same-old—always busy. I must work longer days to make up for the cuts in medical reimbursement. I never get to spend the time with my patients that I would like. Folks are getting older, living longer, and they have different problems; sometimes they just want to talk, and damn it, I just can't sit and talk anymore! They're lonely, their kids are busy working, and some need to be watched like little children. And yet others are very independent and really quite healthy, but they're bored. Then there are the children, and no one likes to see children get sick, and so on. I am just glad I have this retreat at least once a year. I hope you keep this bed and breakfast forever!"

Lillie laughed. "I can't imagine doing anything else." Just then, Amy walked into the kitchen.

"Excuse me, Lillie, have you seen Drew?"

"I think I may have just seen him walking out back in the garden," Lillie responded.

"Oh, thank you. I think we're going to take a walk to the park and check out the theater. Have a good day!" Amy replied, as she proceeded to the garden to meet up with Drew.

"Okay, Amy. Have fun, and I hope we see you at dinner this evening…6 o'clock."

"New guest?" asked Dr. Vic.

"Yes. Half of a real nice couple from Muncie, Indiana. She and her husband have been married for eight years and seem happy. I think they just wanted some time away from the daily routine of life. They came down for breakfast and were both friendly, but quiet. She ate like a little bird; as tiny as she is, there probably isn't room for much food. Come to think of it, he didn't have much of an appetite, either." She paused. "Hmmm…that usually means something is going on. I hope everything is okay. They are so sweet and well suited for one another. I'll have to keep my eye on them." Lillie winked as she reached for the carafe and poured Dr. Vic another cup of coffee. "You probably haven't met any of your housemates yet, have you?"

"As a matter of fact, no, I haven't. But Lillie, you know that's not why I come here. I come here to rest and to eat your delicious food! Oh, and of course, to enjoy your wonderful company."

"Well, you might want to come for dinner tonight at 6 o'clock. One of my guests, Michael Roth, is a regular, and I only make dinner when he is here. He is a writer for a travel magazine and he reports on all different kinds of restaurants. I feel so honored to cook for him;

and besides, I think you will like him and the food! Something tells me the two of you might get along well. Shall I set a place for you?"

"Absolutely, young lady! I would be delighted. I'll even take a shower!"

Lillie laughed again. "Well, that would be real nice, Dr. Vic. See you at six."

Chapter 4

Dr. Vic helped himself to a third cup of coffee and strolled to the front porch where he was greeted by three neighborhood kittens all hoping he had brought them some treats. He reached down and picked up a little black and gray tiger kitty and claimed one of the rocking chairs. Careful to not spill his coffee, he placed the kitten on his lap and proceeded to pet it, and it showed its appreciation by purring as it curled up into a little ball on his lap and became comfortable. The other two kittens were walking back and forth at Dr. Vic's feet, rubbing their backs against his bare legs.

Dr. Vic rocked cautiously in an effort to avoid smashing kitten tails or feet. In his relaxed state, he drifted deep into his thoughts and found himself wondering what his ex-wife might be doing today. Where was she, who was she with, how much of his money was she spending? He started shaking his head as if to rid himself of the thoughts. Then he started thinking about his daughters, all grown up now. He wondered how they were and what important matter kept them from being able to spend time with him on this beautiful weekend.

Before making reservations at *The Lillie Inn*, he had contacted them to see if they might be available for a visit and dinner, but as usual, they were too busy. He had always hoped for a close relationship with them, but how could he have known that his own career would engulf him like a perilous wave that would push him far out to sea? How could he have known that his ex-wife would eventually grow weary of his long hours and the time he spent with his patients, and…the time it took to make more money for her to spend? He devoted his time taking care of others, and she squandered his earnings shopping. "Stupid bitch!" he blurted out loud, and the cute little curled up kitten, then quite startled, jumped with an arched back while the claws of all four paws pierced Dr. Vic's thighs as if to grasp hold for dear life before Dr. Vic tossed it from his lap, watched it fall to the ground and scurry off. His coffee, still hot, shot into the air and landed on his right thigh. He jumped up and attempted to wipe the liquid from his lap, which only made it worse when he rubbed the hot coffee into the fresh, deep claw marks on both thighs.

"What did you do, pinch him?" Maddie asked as she walked out onto the porch.

"Yeah," Dr. Vic replied, "I really want to piss off a cat, with claws, as it sits on the middle of my lap while I'm holding a cup of hot coffee. Now all I have to do is pray it's vaccinated."

Maddie snickered. "I'll get something for you," she said, and she reappeared a minute later with wet paper towels.

"Thanks," he said as he began to wipe his legs, then right arm and hand. "No, really, I was just sitting here thinking, and I didn't realize I was responding out loud to my thoughts. I scared the bejeebers out of the damn kittens and they scared the bejeebers out of me! It's kind of funny...I come here to enjoy the quiet, and in that quiet, I can hear all these noises—these thoughts running wild and out of control inside my head—and well, some of them were just not very pleasant. I'm glad to be distracted from them! I'm Victor Sobiecki, by the way. Everyone calls me Dr. Vic." He reached his hand out to greet Maddie.

"Nice to meet you. I'm Maddie Cowen." She shook his hand. "I came here for the quiet, too. Louisville is a nice city, but…" she paused. "I used to come here often as a child, and I have lots of good memories, which helps keep me from recalling the bad ones."

"Where do you live now, Maddie?" Dr. Vic asked.

"West Virginia."

"Um, are you willing to expand upon that?" he asked.

"Charleston," she responded.

Curious, Dr. Vic continued: "What do you do there? Is your family there? Are you married? Do you have children?"

"Financial analyst, no, no and no." Maddie responded and said nothing more.

"Not much for conversation, are you, Maddie?" Dr. Vic remarked.

"Not when I think you really don't care. Why would I want to share my personal life with someone who is just asking for the sake of making small talk? Well, my personal life isn't just small talk, but it is personal." She had nothing more to say and just sat there. Dr. Vic thought that if she really didn't want to talk, she would get up and walk away, but she didn't. She sat right down in a rocking chair and stared off into space as if Dr. Vic wasn't even there.

"Well, young lady, I may not know about your personal life, but that chip on your shoulder looks pretty heavy. If ya need any help carrying it, let me know. Otherwise, I'll leave you alone with *your* thoughts—and I hope they don't scare you as much as mine scared me." He picked up his empty coffee cup and walked inside. The screen door slammed behind him, and had he turned around, he would have noticed Maddie flinch at the loud noise.

He rinsed his cup, opened the dishwasher and placed it carefully on the top rack. As he closed the door, he looked out the window over the kitchen sink and got a glimpse of Joan in the garden. He noticed her grace as she walked among the flowers and tall grasses. He observed how she bent over to smell each different flower and how the butterflies were attracted to her, just as he, too, suddenly felt attracted to her. He thought about going out to meet her, but she appeared to be enjoying this moment by herself. He then wondered why he wanted to meet her, or why, after all these years, he had any sense of attraction to another woman.

Valerie had pretty much destroyed any illusions he may have had about a long-term relationship with another woman, and he went back to the quiet place where the thoughts just barged right in as if they were expected guests. He could feel his blood pressure start to rise and his face flush as he thought of this woman whom he had come to dislike so immensely. He made a sound of exasperation and shook his head, again as if he could actually shake the thoughts right out of his mind. He turned around to go to his room on the second floor, only to find Lillie had entered the kitchen.

"Well, hello again. How long have you been standing there?" he asked.

"Just long enough to notice you notice Joan in the garden."

"Oh, yes—I noticed. She looks very pleasant and peaceful. I know sometimes looks can be deceiving, but she seems, wise—yes, very wise."

"You sure have that right. Joan has been a guest here off and on for several years, and wise she is. She is a graceful woman filled with wisdom. Would you like to meet her?"

"Oh, no—thanks anyway. I just spilled coffee on my lap a few minutes ago, pissed off a cat, and I think I may have pissed off another one of your guests, too, out on the front porch. I haven't had a shower, and I, uh, don't think I would make a very good first impression. Maybe at dinner…" but just that quickly, Joan came walking in through the back door.

"Hi, Joan!" Lillie greeted. "Have you been enjoying the garden?"

"Yes! It gets lovelier every time I visit. I just came in for a drink of water."

"I'm glad you did—let me get it for you. By the way, have you met your housemate, Dr. Vic?" Lillie handed her a bottle of cold water.

Joan extended her hand and introduced herself: "Joan Jennings," she announced.

"Dr. Vic," he reciprocated. "It's my pleasure."

"What kind of a doctor are you, Dr. Vic?"

"Internist."

"Ah, adult medicine, and you probably spend a lot of time in the hospital."

"Yes, I do—too much time. That's why I'm here this weekend…to get away from all that."

"Don't you enjoy your work—or at least find it rewarding?" Joan asked.

"I do enjoy my work. I find it very important and rewarding; however, it can also be demanding and tiring, so every once in a while, I try to get down here to just rest."

"Good for you," Joan said. "You must take care of yourself, or how could you take care of others? I think a lot of physicians forget self-care."

He nodded, then realized he could think of nothing to say, and he looked around for Lillie to save him, but she had quietly disappeared. "Well, it was nice to meet you, Joan. I have to get in the shower. Will I see you at dinner here this evening?"

"I plan to be there, yes. I'll see you then."

Dr. Vic exited the kitchen. As he walked up the stairs, Michael was walking down. They exchanged greetings, and Dr. Vic disappeared into his room.

Michael had completed his article on *Lynn's* restaurant, and his eyes were tired. He chose to treat himself to a stroll through Central Park, and he was walking toward the front porch as Joan was walking out of the kitchen and in the same direction.

"Well, hello again, Michael."

"Hey, Joan. I finally finished my article, and now I'm headed for a stroll." He opened the door for Joan to step out onto the porch ahead of him.

Maddie was still sitting in the rocking chair, and one of the kittens was curled up on her lap, sleeping soundly. Joan sensed the "chip" on her shoulder.

"Hey, Maddie. Looks like the little kitty likes you," Michael said.

"Yeah, well, she just needed someplace to get comfortable and rest, I guess," she responded.

"You have inspired me Maddie, and I am about to take a walk through the park. I know it's not running, but it's a start. Would you care to join me?" Michael asked.

"Thanks anyway, but I think I have had enough of a workout today."

Michael turned to Joan. "How about you, Joan?"

"Oh no, thank you, but…no. I was up early walking, too. I like to be lazy in the afternoon."

"Okay then, see you in a bit." Michael took off down Belgravia Court.

Joan examined the rocking chairs, as if they were all different, but they weren't. She finally took a seat across from Maddie. "You know, I kind of think he likes you, Maddie."

"Who—Michael? Nah, I doubt it. I have this way of turning men off. I expect he is just being polite."

"I don't think so. Well, I mean he seems like a very nice man—and I happen to know he is single. How about you? Are you single?"

"Oh, yes, I am very single, and frankly, I think I like it like that."

Joan could see that this young lady was a wounded soul. Somewhere, somehow, she had been hurt deeply and now she was very guarded. *Poor dear*, she thought to herself, and she struggled with what to say next when Maddie blurted out, "How can he like me, anyway? He just met me this morning for all of a few minutes! How can you even suggest that?"

"Well, what I meant was that I think he would like to get to know you—yes, I'm certain that is what I meant to say. Of course, he couldn't know you well enough at this point, but Maddie, it might be worthwhile to get to know him. He has had an interesting life, and, my goodness, he is a world traveler! He's not too old and not too young—in fact, by golly, I might consider him for myself if I were considering anyone," and Joan giggled.

"Be my guest, Joan, 'cause I am not interested in getting to know anyone or have anyone get to know me."

"Oh my, Maddie, I have been married twice, and I have grown children—been there, done that! No, I am not seeking that kind of relationship either, and my dear, I am…well, let's just say I am a 'mature' woman with a Medicare ID card," and she raised her eyebrows and winked at Maddie as she minimalized the idea. "Not that Michael would even be interested in a woman thirty years his senior," she said, and her face blushed at the absurd notion. Maddie smiled too.

Joan could see Maddie had a similar thought. "Oh, Maddie, we need to get that thought out of our heads right now! You know, when I was married to my first husband, it was so wonderful for a long time. We laughed and cried together, we had two children together, and I was such a devoted mother. I loved taking care of my kids, being room mother and team mom, and all those great experiences. I loved watching my kids grow up. I became involved in their lives while my husband became involved in his career. Finally, one day we realized how much we had grown apart, and we divorced. It was tough on the kids, but Frank and I weren't angry with each other; we just simply went our separate ways, right under each other's noses.

"The kids did well and soon went off to college—they were practically grown up. But, I missed the companionship of a partner, and it wasn't long before I met another wonderful and fine man. Like myself, he was *mature*, had grown kids and an ex-spouse, and five minutes after we met each other it was clear that we had much in common. We were married six months later, and it was blissful—for about five years…*was* being the key word here. Then I guess he became bored or something, and one day I came home from a weekend away visiting my daughter, and there he was, with another woman. My heart was broken. I thought I would never recover, but I did. Although I do not entertain thoughts of ever getting married again, I have no regrets. I really loved both of my husbands, and I am certain I got the best of both of them. I later learned that the woman who was with my second husband that awful day ended up doing the same to him a year later.

"Every day is a new day, but there was a time when that wasn't so easy for me to say. Early on there were dark days when I felt depressed. I struggled to get out of bed, I didn't answer the phone—hell, I didn't even have a job to go to because both of my husbands were wealthy and I never needed to work. I remember thinking I had nothing to live for...no reason go on, and I considered ending what had become my miserable life. Anyway, that is my sad story, but that was then and is in the past. I am truly a happy person today...I'm happy because I choose to be happy." She smiled.

"So, Maddie, whatever has caused you so much pain, I am sincerely sorry, but I know you can get past it, too." Joan noticed Maddie's eyes tear up. "Good for you, Maddie...let it go...let those tears wash away your pain…let it out." Joan leaned over and touched her knee, just to let her know she was there and she cared.

Maddie threw both hands over her face and started crying, and she cried and cried for ten solid minutes. Joan never moved, staying with her the entire time. Having heard the crying, Lillie came to the door, but she could see that Joan had things under control, and she didn't want to make Maddie any more uncomfortable, so she opened the screen door and handed Joan some tissue, and then, ever so gently, she closed the screen door without making a sound. Joan placed a couple of tissues into Maddie's hands, and Maddie took them and dabbed her face. She took a few more and blew her nose. She cleared her throat and looked up at Joan, and without saying a word, she looked down at her lap, as if embarrassed.

"Doesn't that feel better?" Joan asked. "That is called pain, and crying gets it out of your body so it doesn't hurt so much anymore. You're probably not finished, but that was sure a great beginning. And look— that little kitty hung in there with you the whole time. I know this kitten likes you for sure," Joan said, smiling.

"I need to go wash up, Joan," Maddie said. "I'm sorry for all the emotion."

"Don't you apologize, dear! It is an honor for me to be with you, and I'll be here for you the rest of the weekend if you want to talk some more," Joan replied.

"Thanks, Joan. I'll keep that in mind," Maddie said, before returning to her room.

Joan found herself alone again, and she sat there for a few minutes thinking about Maddie and what could possibly be troubling her so much. Then she started thinking of her own past and the personal things she was so willing to share with Maddie a few minutes prior— private things from her life that had once caused her so much pain. She was proud of how she was able to deal with them after all of these years. Just then, Lillie appeared at the door again. She pushed the screen door open just a little, to make certain she wasn't going to interrupt anything, and when she saw Joan was alone, she stepped out onto the porch.

"How you are doing, Joan?"

"Oh, just fine, dear. You know, we are all pretty much the same. We all have experienced some sort of pain in our lives, and well, I guess Maddie is experiencing some of her own. There is comfort in knowing we're not alone, isn't there?" Joan remarked.

"Oh, yes," Lillie responded. "I remember the days when I was a child, and all that ugliness that went on for so long. There were some good times, too, and I remember thinking that the ugliness would eventually pass, and there would be good times again, but as time went on, it became harder and harder and I began to lose hope. I was glad when Daddy left, but Mama and I were both unhappy for so long, and I knew I would never have the childhood I wanted and deserved. If Daddy had not left, I don't know what would have happened, since I could never have left Mama alone with him. She was so frail. I hated him for the pain he caused, and it is not something I have been able to forget. I'm really grateful to you, Joan, for your help in getting me through some of that hell."

Joan smiled and patted Lillie's knee. "You're doing so well now, too. I'm sorry for your suffering—I'm sorry for anyone's suffering—but the toughest part of emotional pain is not getting through it, you know, always carrying it around like extra baggage."

"You're right. I remember when you first visited the inn, and you were able to read me right away. You could see that I…had issues…more than I knew myself. I haven't forgotten my past, and sometimes it still hurts, but I look at things differently today, and I am able to respond in a different way. I could live forever in misery or I could let it go. My choice! Well, I haven't let all of it go, Joan. I still have work to do, but I'm on the right track." She looked at her watch. "Oh my! I have a meal to prepare, and 6 o'clock will be here before you know it." Lillie reached out to Joan and gave her a hug. "Thanks for being such a good friend, Joan, and thanks for helping Maddie, too." Lillie walked back inside.

Joan resituated herself to become more comfortable in her rocking chair. She pulled a small journal and pen out of the pocket of the oversized sweater she was wearing. She slipped her half-glasses onto her nose, opened her journal and read her last entry, which had been written just before she fell asleep last night. She wrote about how much she enjoyed her visits to the inn and the satisfaction she experienced when meeting new people from different places. Joan was a very spiritual person, and she knew that she was always right where she was supposed to be, doing exactly what she was supposed to be doing. She didn't believe in coincidences, and she was never casual about the acquaintances she made. Every person with whom she made eye contact was important to her.

She started to write her next entry, and it wasn't long before Michael returned. As he walked up the steps to the porch, he greeted Joan. "Anything exciting happen while I was away?" he asked, half-jokingly.

"Not that I am aware of, Michael. Did you enjoy your walk?"

"Indeed. It was nice and relaxing. I think I'll head up for a little rest before dinner. See you soon," He entered the foyer and went up the stairs to the third floor.

Chapter 5

Michael walked to the restroom first, but the door was closed with a sign that read OCCUPIED, so he went into his room across the hall. A few minutes later he poked his head out to see if the bathroom was still occupied, and it wasn't, so he took the opportunity to make use of the facilities. He locked the door behind him, and as he did, he heard doors opening and closing out in the hallway. He couldn't tell from the noise if anyone was coming or going. As far as he knew, Maddie was the only other person on this floor, but the activity sounded like more than one person. He stood there for a moment and listened. It became quiet again, and he dismissed it.

As he turned around, he observed the outstanding and ornate bathroom. Though he had seen this room several times since his arrival, it was surprisingly more striking as the mid-afternoon light entered through the west window and bounced off of the elaborate design and architecture while also creating shadows that brought attention to its beauty. Only natural light made it possible to completely appreciate the marble walls and floor. The gold fixtures of the porcelain tub were striking, and Michael felt a deep appreciation for Lillie and her decorating style. Throughout the entire home, she had restored and enhanced its historical beauty.

Staying at a bed and breakfast was tranquil compared to the bustling atmosphere of high-rise hotels and resorts he had frequented over the years. On the French Riviera, he was a guest at the *Monte Carlo Grand Hotel,* during which time he experienced the delights of Mediterranean cuisine and relaxed by the rooftop pool. His visit was short, but long enough to meet Michelle, who introduced herself as *Mee-shell.* The allure of her French accent was intoxicating, and when she spoke his eyes were fixed on her full lips. She had dark brown hair and eyes, and a curvy figure that was revealed while lounging poolside in a pink bikini. Michael was sure he was out of her league and was pleased just to have been noticed by her.

While in Scotland, Michael had the pleasure of rooming at the *Dalhousie Castle Hotel* in Edinburgh, where he experienced a new and exciting culture of academia, theater, museums and a nightlife that appealed to his age at the time. He appreciated the continuous exposure to mind-stimulating opportunities. Michael knew he was a privileged man, and he was grateful. The diverse cultures he had the opportunity to experience and the acquaintances he made along the way had enriched his life in ways too many to count. But the bed and breakfast on Belgravia Court in Louisville, Kentucky, was a retreat—a warm and quiet hideaway that offered solitude when he wanted it and companionship when, and if, it was his preference.

He took a deep breath and exhaled a heavy sigh as he faced the commode and noticed the entire wall in front of him was a huge mirror. He had noticed it before, but in the afternoon light and the accompanying shadows, it was more obvious. Michael thought it odd that one would have a mirror behind a commode and momentarily felt uncomfortable as he viewed his reflection. He was a strapping man in good form for a late-thirties bachelor, and he began to recall all the years invested in working-out with personal trainers. He knew it would eventually pay off, and he thought that it could quite possibly be the best money he ever spent.

He looked at his face and considered it to be in relatively good condition for a man who had spent a good amount of time in the sun, and his blue eyes were so striking they distracted folks from noticing that his dark chestnut brown hair was thinning just a bit. *Not bad*, he thought to himself, and he flexed his biceps and pectoral muscles, posing. He patted his belly as he realized that it wasn't as toned as it used to be, but he considered it to be reasonably appealing just the same. He couldn't help but notice his most impressive possession, his penis, which had served him well over the years.

Michael recognized he was spending far too much time checking himself out, so he finished his business, washed up and went to his room to take the nap he had promised himself. He was quite tired, and when he lay down on the bed, he thought more of years past, the people who had come and gone, and that he never married. There had been opportunities for marriage, but he never took the plunge, and he never felt the need to explain that to anyone. He had dates when he wanted, and he enjoyed alone time when he had it.

The image of Maddie walking up to her room after her morning jog re-entered his thoughts. Michael recalled how tone and fit she was and admired her athletic prowess. He knew that it required a strong commitment to make ones-self put forth the effort and discipline, and he admired those qualities. His thoughts continued to wander, and before he knew it, he had Maddie completely undressed and in his bed. *Wishful thinking,* he said to himself before he rolled over onto his side and fell asleep.

Chapter 6

When Maddie sat up on her bed, she looked into the mirror of the dressing table across from her. Her hair was tousled, her face blotchy from sobbing and her clothes wrinkled. She felt exhausted from her crying spell on the porch, not to mention a bit embarrassed. It didn't matter that Joan had tried to make her feel less uncomfortable about the whole thing. Maddie was tough. She was careful to protect herself against the possibility of getting hurt. She avoided vulnerable situations at all costs, so she was disappointed with herself this afternoon. She appreciated Joan, but this was the first time she could remember that anyone had seen through her like that and it caught her off guard. *Totally out of character for me,* she thought. She stood up and ran her hands over her face as if to wipe away the blotches. She picked up her hairbrush and ran it through her long, dark hair. She stood staring at herself in the mirror for a moment, knowing it was going to take more than wiping her face and brushing her hair to improve her appearance before dinner.

Maddie opened her door and noticed the restroom was available, so she opted to take a hot bubble bath. She grabbed her bathrobe and toiletries, walked across the creaking landing and into the bathroom, closing the heavy door behind her. She, too, had been captivated by the beautiful, luxurious décor, and she felt quite elegant as she leaned over and turned on the water that flowed with such force it almost frightened her. She added lavender bubble bath to the stream and the room filled with its fragrance. She pulled her hair up, removed all of her clothes, and stepped into the hot bath, easing her way into the fragrant water until she was almost completely immersed. Her head rested comfortably against the curved edge of the tub, and as she closed her eyes, she felt her entire body relax. She was grateful for this moment of pampering and regretted that she didn't take the time to enjoy it more often.

Maddie's thoughts began to wander, and she recalled the conversation she shared with Joan on the porch. She surprised herself at having expressed such emotion with someone who was practically a stranger. She had never met Joan before this weekend, and even if she had known her for years, demonstrating her feelings was definitely not her style. Maddie also thought, however, how comfortable she was with Joan, who certainly didn't seem like a stranger, and she was perplexed by what had come over her.

As she was growing up, Maddie was never able to express her emotion without criticism. It was considered a weakness in her family of conservative educators. Her father was a professor at West Virginia University, and her mother taught high school before she had children and returned to teaching when the children were all in high school themselves. Maddie thought there was absolutely nothing worse than having her own mother teaching at the same school she attended, which she bemoaned on a regular basis. If Maddie had it to do all over again, surely she would have run far, far away, and she began to recall days when she did run away in her thoughts.

Maddie was one of three children, sandwiched between two brothers, Karl and Timothy. She was the only daughter of parents who had lofty expectations and little patience, and although she tried, it seemed that whatever she did, it was never enough. Of course, this was Maddie's opinion, but her perception was her reality.

Karl, her older brother, was the "finest son" a man could ever wish for. He could do no wrong. He was well-behaved throughout his childhood, earned excellent grades, and graduated with honors from the College of William and Mary. Growing up in Karl's shadow was made easier only because he really was as good as everyone thought. He was always there for Maddie, without exception. He could help her with any homework assignment, and he did so without complaining. If she had a problem with a friend, Karl would listen and give support; he never told her what to do or that she was silly for having the problem in the first place, though looking back, Maddie could see how ridiculous many of them were.

Karl was always her protector. Every boyfriend had to endure an "inquisition" prior to her dating him, and though it embarrassed her then, Maddie learned to be grateful for his concern. Yes, Karl was next to perfect…right down to the way he looked: tall and strikingly handsome with dark brown hair and deep blue eyes. He was the focus of many young women, and Maddie knew that there were older girls at school who only wanted to be her friend because it might enhance their chances of meeting Karl. Maddie didn't mind: she enjoyed the attention.

Karl had just earned his law degree when he came home one warm Friday in June. His favorite meal had been prepared, and his bedroom looked just the way he left it after the previous Christmas holiday. The final months of school kept him too busy for visits since then, but it was a worthwhile sacrifice, to complete his education at the top of his class. He had been wined and dined by some of the most reputable law firms in the country, and he was pleased to inform his folks that he had accepted an offer.

There was a lot of commotion when Karl arrived. The family had not enjoyed a meal together since the last time he was home, and it gave his parents great pleasure to have them all together again. Dinner conversation was filled with everyone sharing the most recent activities of their lives.

Maddie was telling Karl of all the girls who had been calling, anxious to know of Karl's availability. Karl enjoyed the flattery. He sat back in his chair, sipping the coffee his mother had just poured. He discussed his pending job with a law firm in West Virginia, and that he would be sitting for the state bar exam in July. The family was thrilled, knowing he would remain close, both figuratively and literally. Following dinner, Maddie and her mother cleared the table while Karl, Timothy and their dad retreated to the family room. Maddie and her mother soon joined them, and before anyone knew it, it was midnight, as indicated by the twelve commanding gongs from the clock. With that, the whole family said their goodnights and retired.

They all slept in on Saturday morning, eventually awakened by the barking dogs next door. These dogs never allowed the neighbors to sleep in too late on any given day, though it felt most unfair on Saturdays. Soon, they were all up and bustling around. Karl asked Maddie to go shopping with him to purchase new clothes for his new job. She was both flattered and excited. She loved to shop, but more importantly, she was so fond of her brother, and that he would ask for her help was a huge compliment to her. She looked forward to it. She informed Karl that it was going to be a long day, and the earlier they got started, the better. By 11 o'clock that morning they were off to the mall and specialty stores. Back home, Maddie's mother was busy with Saturday chores, and her father was fiddling around in his office.

Timothy started his day tending to the lawn, a chore that he truly enjoyed, though he didn't want anyone to know it. He would always act like it was an imposition, because he thought that if his parents knew how much he disliked the "chore," they would be easier on him the rest of the day. The truth was, he appreciated the opportunity to be in solitude during grass cutting, and it gave him the opportunity to plan his entire weekend. When he was finished, he admired his work and accepted all acclaims for the lovely lawn.

As Maddie and Karl were en route to the mall, she ran down a list of all the places they needed to stop, including men's specialty stores, where they would inspect tailor-made suits. Maddie was excited for her brother, and she was equally proud to be a part of developing his professional image. The time went quickly, and they had made only a few purchases before they realized it was 2 o'clock and they had not yet eaten lunch.

"How about a food break, Maddie?" Karl asked.

"Sounds great," she responded, and they pulled into a nearby restaurant. Not long afterward, they were back on the shopping trail, and they didn't head for home until they had purchased seven suits with matching shirts, ties, and socks, three pairs of shoes, and two belts. The suits were all left at the stores for alterations, and Karl was to pick them up in two weeks. It felt good to Karl to have this mission accomplished, and he was grateful to his sister for her help.

Karl began to tease her.

"So, Maddie...didn't you have something better to do on a Saturday than hang out with your brother?"

"Of course I did, but I felt sorry for you, and there is no way I could trust you to successfully accomplish this task alone. I don't want to be embarrassed because your clothes don't match!" She and Karl both laughed.

Maddie was completely relaxed in the bubble bath as she remembered that morning with her brother. Her eyes were closed, and she wore a look of contentment. But, as Maddie's mind continued to wander, her expression changed, recollecting the rest of that Saturday in June.

Karl asked, "Is there anything you want to do before we go home, Maddie?"

"Not really, but could we stop and get some ice cream for dessert tonight? I'm having a craving and we've certainly earned it after this long day of shopping."

The only store between their current location and home was the next left turn, and Karl quickly changed lanes to enter the parking lot. Maddie heard some excitement, and that's all she remembered until she woke up in the emergency room.

As she sat in the tub surrounded by bubbles, her eyes suddenly shot wide open, trying to halt the memories in her head—the memories of the day she wished she could have back.

Maddie remembered opening her eyes in the hospital, although she couldn't really make anything out. Everyone and everything was a blur. She started moaning and complaining that her back hurt. "Mommy," she whined as if she were a five-year-old. "Mommy? Daddy?" Then her eyes opened wide and she screamed "Karl! Oh my God—oh my God! Karl! Karl!" and quickly she was asleep again. She had been sedated.

Several days later, she awoke in the hospital to see her mother and father standing next to her. "Maddie, Sweetie, Mommy and Daddy are here. Hi, Honey." and she felt her mother's hand touch her forehead. It was a comfortable touch, and she felt safe. Maddie drifted in and out for the next couple of days while her mother and father stayed at her side. Six days had passed before Maddie was coherent.

"What happened, Mommy?" Maddie asked. Her mother bolted from the chair she had fallen asleep in.

"Maddie! Maddie! Hello, Dear!" Her mother was ecstatic to see her awake. It was rare that Maddie's mother was ever that excited. The more awake Maddie became, the more confused she was. She viewed her unfamiliar surroundings and heard unfamiliar voices.

"You were in an accident, Sweetie—a terrible accident—but you're going to be fine…you're going to be just fine." Her mother sounded reassuring, but Maddie saw tears in her eyes. Her mother reached over and pushed the call button on Maddie's bedside. "She's awake! She's awake!" she exclaimed, and soon a nurse entered into the room along with Maddie's father.

"Hello, Dear," the nurse greeted, and Maddie's father reached down to touch Maddie's face.

"Hello, Kitten," he said.

"What happened? What's going on?"

"You're in the hospital, Maddie…do you remember anything about how you got here?" the nurse asked.

"No…I mean…" and she paused as her eyes moved back and forth trying to put everything together. "No!" I don't remember!" She became very frustrated.

The nurse stroked her arm, and checked her IV, "it's okay, Maddie. Calm down."

"Maddie, Dear," her mother said, "You and Karl were in a terrible accident…the day you were shopping for his new work clothes…do you remember?"

"Oh, yes! We just did that—we just went shopping!" She started putting pieces together.

"It was several days ago, Sweetie—in fact, it was six days ago."

"Mommy, what is going on?"

"Oh, Maddie, I don't know exactly what happened, but you and Karl were in a car accident on your way home from your shopping trip."

"How is Karl, Mommy?" Her mother's eyes filled with tears. The nurse standing next to her was administering medication into Maddie's IV.

"Karl…Karl didn't make it, Maddie." She began crying out loud. "He's gone, Maddie…our Karl is dead."

As Maddie sat in the bubble bath, consumed by memories of the saddest day of her life, tears streamed down her face, now flushed and swollen. She cried until she couldn't cry any more. She loved Karl…she missed him so much…he was good and smart and handsome…everyone loved Karl, and Maddie thought she loved him most of all. Having to live the rest of her life without him seemed almost impossible. Maddie cried until her tear ducts went dry; she hadn't even noticed the bath water had turned cold and the bubbles had melted away.

She slid her body forward until her head was submerged in the bath water, and as she shivered, goose bumps covered her skin. She held her breath as long as she could, wishing, like so many times before, that she had the courage to stay under the water until Karl came to get her.

She came to her senses and thrust her body up out of the water, soon standing up and dripping all over the floor. She grabbed the towel and wrapped herself in it, then grabbed another and started drying herself. She viewed her reflection and swollen face, and although it was painful to relive her past, she felt a sense of release, of letting go; she thought she may even look better, swollen face or not. Maddie brushed her teeth and combed her wet hair back. She flipped the fan switch so the moisture would clear. The room still smelled of fresh lavender, and as she breathed in the scent, she relaxed and felt lighter.

Maddie put on the terrycloth robe hanging on the back of the door. She gathered her personal items, reached for the crystal doorknob, and opened the heavy door only to look up and make direct eye contact with Michael, who was headed downstairs. Maddie's head turned downward in embarrassment, but not before Michael realized she had been crying.

"Maddie," he said softly, "are you alright?"

Wishing he hadn't noticed, she nodded.

He wanted to reach out and touch her; she seemed fragile. Earlier that day she was stoic and strong, even after running until she was exhausted and breathless. Her body was firm and resilient, but now she looked like a vulnerable little girl as she shuffled across the landing in her slippers.

Michael felt a profound sense of sadness rush through him as he watched her open the door and enter her room. Maddie could see a compassionate, thoughtful, and caring man with a sensitivity she hadn't noticed when watching him devour more pancakes this morning than she could eat in a month. Now she saw someone different—someone who could wrap her in his arms and protect her from the pain of the world.

"Maddie?" Michael said, but she didn't budge. "Maddie…are you alright?"

Maddie forced a small but sad smile and nodded to Michael, "Yeah, I'm alright," she said. "I…I have a lot on my mind."

"Well, if there is anything I can do, Maddie, I am here," Michael responded.

"I appreciate that, Michael. You are very kind. I—well, I—damn-it—I..." and she started crying again.

She didn't notice Michael had approached her until he touched her shoulders with both hands and drew her near. When she didn't back away, Michael wrapped his arms around her, pulled her in, and she buried her head in his massive chest and cried. Michael knew there was nothing he could say. When he breathed the lavender scent in, it brought peace to the moment. Michael embraced this beautiful woman whom he had admired from the moment he first saw her.

Maddie became more calm and relaxed until her crying soon stopped. She used the sleeve of her robe to wipe her face and her runny nose. She gently pushed herself away from Michael, but his arms were still wrapped around her. He didn't want to let go, and she didn't want him to, either.

"I'm so sorry," she said.

"Please don't be," Michael responded. "I am sorry. I am sorry for your pain and sadness, and I wish that I could help. Is there anything I can do?" he asked.

"There is nothing anyone can do, Michael, but I appreciate that you would want to. My sadness is about something that is already done, and I have to learn to live with it."

"Do you want to talk about it?" Michael asked, and Maddie surprised herself when she said that she did. She invited Michael into her room.

She had completely forgotten that she wasn't even dressed. The room was beautiful, with a huge, red cherry bed covered with blue-flowered bedding that matched the canopy. There was a night table on either side of the bed, each occupied by a lamp with matching blue-flowered shades. Off to one side of the bed were French doors that opened onto a lovely balcony surrounded by a wrought-iron railing. On the other side of the room were two wing-back chairs separated by an antique red cherry end table that also displayed a blue-flower-shaded lamp, and Michael sat in one of the chairs. Maddie placed her items on a dressing table. As she poured herself a glass of water, she offered one to Michael, who accepted. The only light in the room shone through the window. Maddie curled up into the chair on the other side of the table, took a drink of water and proceeded to tell Michael the entire story of her brother. It took some time, and occasionally her eyes became teary, but when the story was told, she felt better. He felt profound sadness for her.

Michael's hand was resting on the table that separated the two chairs. Maddie reached for her glass and took a drink. As she returned it to the table, Michael reached for her hand and held it gently in his.

"I am so sorry, Maddie. I don't know what to say. I'm glad you shared this with me. You have been carrying this burden for so long. I wish I could tell you of a way to make your pain go away—a way to make it disappear, or better yet, I wish I could bring Karl back to you. I don't know why it is that some folks go through life with apparent ease while others must suffer."

Maddie noticed Michael's eyes tear up.

"I didn't mean to upset you, Michael. I—well, you were here, and I was ready. You're right, I have been carrying this burden for so long, almost ten years, and the pain has been heavy. That's why I run, you know: every time I run, I think of Karl and that day and my folks and the tragedy. Sometimes I really do believe I can run away from it. Since then, I have never let anyone get close. I lost my brother—the light of our family. My parents haven't been the same, and my other brother moved away. I don't understand it—I guess we just couldn't deal with it. I talk with my parents every now and then, but I think they hold me responsible, though they never said that. I just…well, it's just a feeling I get. Maybe it's me, I don't know…but I think my whole family is just too afraid now to be close—too afraid it might happen again."

She noticed her tiny hand enveloped by Michael's big and protective hand.

"I've never told this to anyone, Michael—never shared my personal life like this. I don't know what's gotten into me. Karl was such a beautiful person…it seems so wrong for him to be gone. Life without him has been difficult for me and my whole family…I don't know how to move on."

Maddie became silent. Without realizing it, her fingers worked their way through Michael's until they became completely entwined. Michael rose from his chair, never letting go of Maddie's hand, and tears were still wet in his eyes. He knelt down in front of Maddie, and with her hand encased in his, he gently placed it on her lap.

"I am so very sorry, Maddie—I don't know what to say."

"What can anyone say?" Maddie replied. "This is just something I need to work through—and someday I will, I hope." She managed a little smile.

Michael stood up in front of Maddie and reached out for her. Without words, she understood his intention, and she rose. She reached up and wiped the tears from Michael's eyes.

"Thank you for caring, Michael, and thank you for listening."

Michael put his other hand around her tiny shoulders, pulled her in close to him and held her quietly. His chest was heavy with the sadness that he felt for her, but he knew this was all he could do, and that it was enough for now.

She rested her head against his chest again, and for the first time in years, she felt safe and warm and cared for. She closed her eyes, took a deep breath and let it go. After a minute, she pulled herself away only slightly, and looked up at Michael's face. She saw tenderness and thoughtfulness in his face.

Michael didn't want anything except to make Maddie feel better. She was beautiful, he thought. Her face glowed, with her rosy cheeks and glassy eyes.

Maddie was the first to speak.

"You know, Michael, I feel better—really, I do. I can't explain it, and I almost feel guilty about it, but I do feel better."

Michael guided her now-dry hair away from her face. Without hesitation, Maddie reached her arms around his neck, stood on her toes and kissed his lips with tenderness and passion. Michael reciprocated, and without their lips separating, Michael picked Maddie up and sat her on the bed. She never let go of him. He sat next to her and pulled away, breaking the kiss. He looked into Maddie's eyes, asking if she wanted him to stop, and clearly she did not. He lifted her up and placed her head on the pillow. Maddie said nothing. She reached for him again, and Michael came closer and kissed her lips. Both Maddie and Michael were experiencing feelings not felt in a long time.

Maddie had not realized her subconscious longing for intimacy—not just the fulfillment of touching and desire, but also the compassionate understanding and thoughtfulness a close relationship offers. She had been lonely and miserable; living with guilt and denying herself pleasure for so long. Now Maddie found herself releasing all of her pent-up anger, and it felt very, very good, and she was embracing the moment without caution.

Michael had his frustrations, too. It had been a long time since he had been with a woman, and with the exception of one serious relationship long ago, the rest had been forgotten for their insignificance. They were empty, fleeting moments of his past, too many to remember.

Michael had never felt like he was feeling in this moment. He cared for Maddie. He wanted to erase her sadness, and he cared about her pain. He felt strong next to Maddie, who was so fragile and vulnerable, and he knew she wasn't thinking clearly. In his heart, he knew that making love to her now, in this moment, was not right.

Maddie was special. Her life had been difficult, and Michael knew that to take her now would be to take advantage of her vulnerability, and while there was a time when that would not have stopped him, Maddie was different, and he couldn't do it. He couldn't risk her waking up tomorrow with more regrets. It felt good to Michael to care that much and to have a level of respect for a woman whom he knew for such a short time. Lying next to her, Michael cradled Maddie in his arms, pulling her closer. She felt safe, and time stood still. Michael watched Maddie fall asleep. He felt her chest rise and fall with each breath. He felt his own vulnerability, too. He took another deep breath and held on.

Maddie looked peaceful as she slept. In the quiet, Michael heard noises again, like someone right outside the door—or was it next door? He held his breath as he listened, and the sounds ended as quickly as they had started.

Chapter 7

Andrew sat on the balcony overlooking the back of the inn. He watched the colorful autumn leaves falling from the ginkgo tree along with the occasional splat of a ginkgo fruit. Andrew laughed at the contradiction of this handsome, picturesque tree, revered by some and despised by others. On the one hand, it offers shade and protection and is a symbol of great strength. On the other, without regard for its surroundings, it drops its sticky seeds to rot on the ground. Happy he was up far enough to avoid the stench of the malodorous fruit, Andrew plopped his legs on the wicker table and rested his head against the back of the rocker. He closed his eyes and tried to relax as he considered how he might tell Amy the truth; how he might mimic the strength of the gingko tree.

Andrew loved Amy. He loved the way she walked. He loved her long, golden hair. He loved the way she adored him and how she pampered him. She was so young and beautiful when he met her many years ago. She still looked young and beautiful, and Andrew found it hard to believe they had been married eight years already. While the time seemed to go fast in many ways, each day felt longer as Andrew avoided telling Amy what he knew he must.

Andrew reminisced about his high school days when he was popular and every girl in the school considered him the best catch. It was a tiny school in a rural town in Southern Indiana, where Andrew was a big fish in a small pond, and he loved it. By the time he graduated, he had dated about every girl in his class as well as a few in the underclass. He managed to earn good marks academically, as well, and while he wasn't much of an athlete, he did letter in track. Andrew could run! His long, slender body was solid muscle, and he ran with such grace and ease, it almost didn't look like running at all. Girls would swoon at track meets and applaud his triumphs as if he had just won an Olympic medal.

Andrew's accomplishments were far more impressive than those of any of his classmates, and it challenged Andrew to not let all this popularity go to his head. In his senior year, he was offered three scholarships to colleges in big cities and far away from this small Indiana town. He spent much of his final year visiting campuses and exploring his options. He already knew he was a good catch and enjoyed playing the field and keeping everyone at bay. He was borderline arrogant but somehow he managed to charm his way into every girl's heart, and mothers adored him. The dean was proud to consider him one of his own successes, and it was obnoxious how the teachers drooled over him.

When Amy met Drew, she fell madly in love, like all the other girls, but only she was able to win his love in return. As Drew was sought-after by women, Amy was the target of most of the guys. Amy was not as academically nor athletically inclined, but she was beautiful and most charming. Amy's greatest aspiration, nonetheless, was to capture the heart of Drew and make him her own.

Andrew and Amy were young when they first met. They didn't know what they didn't know, and no one was going to tell them what they didn't know. While the parents had no real problem with either Amy or Drew, when they saw that the two were getting serious in high school, they tried to discourage them. It was to no avail, and Amy and Drew became inseparable the summer after graduation. They had become a well-known couple, and everyone wanted to be their friend.

Amy and Drew graduated from high school with wonderful memories, and both went on to college, together. They graduated, started great careers, and were married in an elaborate ceremony. There had been constant excitement in their lives, always something wonderful to look forward to. Eight years later, though, their lives were changing—the way all lives change over time.

Amy and Drew had already achieved many of their goals, and the only thing they longed for now was a child. For many years they hoped it would just "happen," but it never did...until now. Amy was waiting for the perfect moment to share her good news with Drew—to tell him that her doctor confirmed just last week that she is eight weeks pregnant. So far he hadn't even noticed her "glow," and he had also not noticed her morning sickness, which actually had not been too bad. She hadn't gained any weight at all, still looking svelte as ever. And although it was all she could do to contain her excitement, she wanted this special moment to be perfect. She became lost in her thoughts as she imagined Drew's joyful response to her news.

Andrew walked in from the balcony, catching Amy off-guard for a moment.

"Are you ready for dinner?" he asked.

"I will be in a few minutes. Are you okay?"

"Yes," he said.

Amy knew he wasn't, and she realized that he had been acting different for some time. *Or was it her imagination*, she wondered. She went into the dressing room to freshen up for dinner. As she stood in front of the mirror, she began pondering how she would tell Drew, and she decided it would be tomorrow morning before breakfast, so they could share the news with their new friends at the inn, or maybe tonight after dinner, when they were alone.

Drew realized how important it was to tell Amy his news, and he didn't feel good about putting it off any longer. He didn't want to ruin dinner for Amy, and she had been in such good spirits lately. *Tomorrow*, he thought—*I'll tell her in the morning*. He started pacing the room. "*No time is a good time. I'm going to ruin everything for Amy and for us. I have to tell her. I can't keep putting it off!! But no matter when or how I do this, it's gonna be bad!* His heart started racing. For six weeks he had been contemplating how he would break this news. He was distracted from everything—from his work, from running, from his coaching at the high school, and…from Amy. He just wanted his *news* to go away.

"What a mess," he said out loud without even realizing it.

"What?" Amy asked.

"What?" Drew asked in return.

"What did you say…something about a mess?"

"Oh." He began mumbling, "Oh, I uh—I was just thinking about something I need to do, and I guess I was thinking out loud," he said. "You ready?"

"Yep!" Amy announced as she walked out of the bathroom.

"You look beautiful, Amy."

"Really? Why, thank you. It seems like you haven't noticed me at all recently." She planted a little kiss on his cheek as they walked out the door.

Chapter 8

Dr. Vic couldn't get enough sleep, the only guilty pleasure he allowed himself. Life as an internist isn't like it used to be. These days he found himself working longer hours for a lot less revenue. He had to hire new people in his office to deal with the ever-growing list of new regulations and forms. He loathed that he had to spend less time with his patients because he had to hurry from one to the next. Every day was a challenge, and as he was getting older, it was even harder to keep up. On more than one occasion, he contemplated giving up medical practice altogether. He considered research or consulting or even working for a pharmaceutical company as a rep, but those thoughts would soon dissipate as he recalled his patients through the years, the relationships he developed, and the satisfaction he felt when he helped others.

These people had come to depend on him, and he was now treating multi-generations of families. The nurses at the hospital appreciated Dr. Vic and his devotion to his patients. He worked long days and nights, even when he wasn't on call, and he would simply find a place to rest in the hospital—usually the cafeteria or one of the patient lounges. He was a truly dedicated and diehard patient advocate, although the hospital occasionally had a tough time with him when new compliance requirements were established.

Change didn't come easy for Dr. Vic, especially when it meant it might make life harder for his patients. He defied rules that, in his opinion, were put into place only to save money for the multimillion-dollar insurance industry. He had no pity for them, and he made no bones about it. He would probably be angry anyway, but when one of his patients died of a perforated appendix twenty-five years ago because he couldn't get the insurance company to authorize a visit to the emergency room, Dr. Vic went ballistic.

He had cared for this man for years, as well as his wife, mother and children. If it had been a weekday, maybe the outcome would have been different, but it was late on Saturday when he called his insurance company to get authorization to go to the ER. By the time they authorized the visit on Monday, his patient had died. "Insane!" he exclaimed over and over. It was a difficult time for him and his patient's family, and ever since, he just couldn't accommodate the will of what he referred to as *mismanaged-managed-care.*

That was a long time ago, when Dr. Vic was relatively new in practice. He was married to his high school sweetheart, Valerie, and they had two young daughters. He didn't learn until it was too late how hard his wife worked to take care of him and the girls. He was rarely home, and she was lonely. The little girls missed their daddy when he was gone for long periods of time, and his wife longed for him, too.

He missed his family as well, but he had accepted his responsibilities long ago, and to him it meant putting his patients first. That is not to say he didn't have needs and desires of his own. Being the hero doctor that he appeared to be, getting *his needs* satisfied was never a problem. Every nurse in the hospital would have been willing to put this doctor to bed every night. Then, one day when Valerie was feeling particularly lonely, yearning for her husband and weary from spending too much time alone with their two daughters, she made a plan—one that was subsequently detailed in court documents.

She called her trustworthy babysitter who agreed to watch the girls. She prepared a basket with two char-grilled Porterhouse steaks, twice-baked potatoes, green bean casserole, salad and bread, and drove to the hospital. She knew that Vinney, as she endearingly referred to him, would either be in the medical staff on-call room or seeing a patient somewhere else on the unit. Either way, he would be surprised, especially when she arrives and removes her coat to reveal the peach lace teddy she was wearing underneath. She smiled to herself both in anticipation of her expectations and her creativity.

Valerie had never done anything like this before, though she wondered why. She knew the hospital provided rooms for physicians on the call roster for respite, and she had visited Vinney there before, although the circumstances were different. She also realized that Vinney may not be available, and if that was the case, she intended to leave the basket of food and save the teddy for another occasion.

Valerie was anxious as she placed the basket in the car. She would have included a bottle of wine if Vinney weren't on call. It was a fifteen-minute drive to the hospital, and she had been anticipating this the entire day. She went to the spa and had her hair styled and got a facial. She was wearing his favorite cologne, which he bought her for her birthday last year.

On the drive to the hospital Valerie started to get cold feet. She was excited by the risk she was taking, but what if Vinney was busy with a patient, or worse, what if he got mad at her for pulling a crazy stunt? She had not even considered possible negative outcomes when she was busy concocting her adventure. She relaxed when she remembered Vinney was on call for inpatient emergencies only, which he had once told her were few and that he spent most of his time on administrative duties and medical records, especially on weeknights.

Valerie regained her confidence and accepted that while her effort may be for naught, it was worth a try.

When she arrived, she could see from a distance that most of the lights in the hospital had been dimmed. She parked her car in the garage, grabbed her basket and took the crosswalk to the hospital. She didn't pass too many people, and those she did barely noticed her.

She knew several of the nurses on the unit; they called her home almost every day, but she hoped that none of them would notice her. Valerie really wanted to surprise her tired, overworked and dedicated husband. The halls were quiet when she passed a resident she recognized who was serving a Night's rotation. He acknowledged her, and she nodded back. He likely noticed the smell of her cologne as she breezed past him. He turned around and watched her as she disappeared down the hall.

Valerie approached the nurse's station where the staff was busy taking care of business. One of the nurses noticed Valerie and acknowledged her as she went from one task to another. It wasn't uncommon for spouses to visit, and the nurse thought nothing of it. It was almost 8 o'clock. Valerie hoped she arranged her visit at a time convenient for Vinney. Shift changes should have already occurred, and patients would have finished their dinner and received their evening meds. While this was a significant risk for the otherwise modest and cautious Valerie, she determined the effort was worth it.

She walked down the hall to the call room and knocked on the closed door. When there was no answer, she opened it slowly, poked her head in, and scanned the dark room, which was slightly illuminated by the dim glow of the EXIT sign from above the door. She placed the basket on the floor, out of the way, and tiptoed toward the bulge under the bedcovers. She reached to peak under the covers, when behind her the bathroom door opened, and out walked her naked husband.

"Vinney," she said almost inquisitively. "Geeze, you scared me!"

"Baby, is that you?" he asked.

Valerie immediately realized the bulge remained in the bed while her husband stood naked in the doorway of the bathroom. She looked down at the protrusion and grasped the covers. Vinney tried to reach for her before she could pull them off, but he wasn't fast enough. She plucked the covers from the bed and found a terrified

Lisa Monroe staring back at her. Lisa was a nurse she had known for years. Valerie felt the fury begin to build within her. Her heart was racing, her head was spinning and her ability to reason became incapacitated. She took a deep breath and laid into Vinney.

"Oh my God! Oh my God, Vinney! What the hell! Oh my God!"

Her arms were flailing, tossing the sheet that only a moment ago covered the nurse who had been sleeping with her husband for who knows how long.

"Vinney…how could you?" she screamed.

Vinney took her in his arms and tried to pull her closer and calm her down, "Baby—oh God, I am so sorry, Baby!"

As hard as he tried, her arms kept flailing and her legs were kicking aimlessly.

"Do not touch me, you pig! Back away from me! I hate you!"

Lisa crunched herself up into a little ball at the head of the bed, her eyes searching rapidly for her clothes as she tried desperately to grab something to cover herself.

Vinney continued his efforts to calm down his wife, while Lisa searched for a way out of the bed and into the bathroom. She finally managed to get her hands on Vinney's shirt that was lying on the floor and wrapped it around her. Her head was buzzing with a million thoughts, not the least of which was why she allowed herself to say yes to this in the first place! The crawl toward the bathroom seemed like a mile as she was trying to avoid the aimless kicking of Valerie, for whom she actually felt sorry. She never even thought of her while she was sleeping with her husband, which she had done many times before, and as far as she knew, it was the best kept secret in the hospital.

Only two feet to the bathroom and suddenly, WHAM! Someone threw open the door to the room and whacked her right in the ass! The nursing supervisor, who was responding to the commotion, had been a little too anxious to see what was going on. Stunned is what she was; totally stunned! Standing in front of her was an unclothed Dr. Vic, trying desperately to calm his infuriated wife, who by now didn't look as pretty as when she arrived. Her hair was tousled, and her makeup was smeared. She had one shoe on and no idea as to the location of the other. A few buttons from her coat had popped off, allowing it to hang open, exposing her not quite as pretty peach teddy. And on the floor was Lisa, looking like a twenty-eight-year-old toddler crawling on the floor, also naked with the exception of the shirt that barely covered anything.

"Do I need to call security, or would you rather that no one else be involved with this little matter right now?" The night supervisor's voice was as clear as her message.

Valerie finally gave up her fight pushing Dr. Vic as far away from her as possible in the small room. He reached over for the sheet that was now lying on the bed and held it in front of him. Lisa managed to crawl the distance into the bathroom, and quietly closed the door.

The supervisor spoke in a quiet yet firm tone to avoid disturbing others, but loud enough to make herself very clear.

"I don't know what is going on, and I don't need to know, but whatever it is, it must stop, and it must stop now. This is a hospital."

Then she walked over to the bathroom door, carefully pushed it open and said "Lisa, you're fired. Get dressed and get out!"

She looked at Dr. Vic and said, "We'll talk later."

She then looked at Mrs. Sobiecki and asked, "Is there anything I can do for you?"

"No…thank you."

Mrs. Sobiecki caught sight of her lost shoe, leaned over to pick it up and slid it onto her foot. She pulled her coat closed, picked up her basket, and walked straight for the door. Without turning around, devastated and distraught, she hurried out of the room.

The nursing supervisor hurried to the phone, called security and told them to look for a woman with a basket leaving the Med-Staff Unit, headed for the garage, and to make sure she safely reached her car. She returned to the Call Room, stood resolute in front of Dr. Vic and demanded:

"Get your naked ass dressed and take it home. There's probably nothing left of your marriage after this, but don't let that woman go home and deal with this herself. I'll call Dr. Braden and let him know you have a family emergency. I'm sure he'll take call the rest of the night." Disgusted, she started to walk out of the room. She stopped, turned back toward him and added:

"I don't know how often this has happened—you taking advantage of my nurses—but you have no right. This is a hospital—you are a doctor. This isn't over." She turned back around and walked away.

Lisa got dressed. In complete humiliation, she walked through the halls of the hospital to the employee exit that led to the parking garage. She had hoped no one noticed her disposition and was grateful that at this hour, there weren't many people around. She was too mortified to even ask security to walk her to her car, and if she had a prayer left, she prayed that Valerie didn't run her over as she was leaving the garage. On the other hand, she didn't really care if she did.

Dr. Vic was numb. Looking like a pathetic, washed-up whore, he stood there naked, wondering what he had done—how in an instant he had destroyed his marriage, subjected his children to years of therapy, ruined the reputation and livelihood of a nurse, and caused such a distraction in the hospital, it would be the main topic of conversation for months to come.

The sun did rise and fall every day after that, but Dr. Vic fell into a depression he could have never imagined. He and, the now ex, Mrs. Sobiecki, experienced a painful divorce, the girls did end up in therapy, and it wasn't long before Dr. Vic became estranged from them all. He had made a horrible mistake, and he was certain he would never be forgiven.

As the years went by, Valerie took advantage of her position as the wronged wife of a physician, the victim of adultery, suffering the humiliation of public betrayal, not to mention her shattered dreams. Now she was alone with two disturbed children whose father was now more absent than before. She portrayed her new character well, and it wasn't long before Dr. Vic knew that he could either fight her or give in. He was too busy fighting for lives in the hospital, and he gave in to Valerie's demands. And why wouldn't he? No one blamed Valerie, after all. She was encouraged to take what she could get, so she took the house, the BMW, the bling-bling that no longer had meaning, and the gym membership. She left her ex-favorite cologne.

The few pleasures Dr. Vic did allow himself these days included the few quiet weekends every year he could fit into his busy schedule, busier now that he was the ex-husband of a woman who seemed to take immense pleasure in what now seemed her life's mission to make him miserable. He was always looking for some distraction and what was better than working day and night to make the money he needed to support his ex-wife and daughters? He decided long ago that being married with two children was definitely less expensive than being divorced with two children. Nonetheless, here he was today, at the inn with these people whom he will probably never see again and wondering if he really cared about having dinner with them.

Chapter 9

Dr. Vic's room was decorated in dark cherry wood furniture and forest green linens. In one corner and next to the fireplace was a large leather recliner where he took a seat. He could not have cared less about the décor, though he found the room to be comfortable, and he wondered if he would like it as much if it had been decorated in pink. It was a fleeting moment. He was pretty well rested by now, and his mind was definitely wandering.

He turned his head toward the window and noticed that the day was coming to an end. It was a sobering moment, reminding him of when he was a child and he had nothing to do. He had strived to get away from all the noise and daily hassles of life, and now he found himself bored! He began to emotionally kick himself in the ass.

"Damn it," he said out loud, "I need to get a life!" He forced the lever on the side of the chair down, and his feet dropped to the floor. He stood up and looked out the window. It was a beautiful fall evening and it had been a beautiful fall day, *and I missed it*, he realized. His thoughts were running rampant. *I've been here before, tired and restless, ugh…I can't stand it anymore!*

He went into the bathroom and turned on the shower. Steam soon filled the room, and he stripped naked and stepped under the force of the nozzle as if to wash his troubles away. He stayed in the shower a good twenty minutes before he started to run out of hot water, when he shut it off. He patted himself dry, wrapped the towel around his waist and lathered his face for a good, old-fashioned shave. He brushed his teeth, combed his hair and dressed in a nice pair of khakis, a shirt and pullover sweater. Before he knew it, the clock gonged six times. He looked approvingly at himself in the mirror, then turned around, slipped his feet into a pair of loafers and walked toward the door. His attention was drawn to the dresser, which reminded him to splash on a bit of cologne. He took the hint, smiled, and as he prepared to go downstairs for dinner, he remembered he told Joan he would see her there—and his smile grew.

Chapter 10

The mouthwatering aroma of dinner filled the air, and memories began flowing through Lillie's mind as if they were attached to the smells. She believed she would never tire of cooking, and she was continuously gathering new recipes and new dishes in which to serve them. Lillie was endearing to many of her guests, and several of them enjoyed adding to her collection of serving dishes. This night she knew she wanted to serve her mother's favorite glazed carrot recipe in the porcelain dish her guest, Mrs. Richardson, presented to her at her last visit.

This evening was one of the rare occasions that Lillie would prepare dinner, and she wanted it to be perfect. Cozy and comfy would be the theme of the evening. Lillie would make every effort to assure her guests felt welcome as they arrived at the table, and no detail would be overlooked.

As Lillie prepared the menu, she also took into consideration the serving pieces for each item. She did this intentionally since every serving piece had a story, and if ever the guests were at a loss for conversation, Lillie could always share an enchanting tale of a piece of china that most everyone found enjoyable. She would usually have to share only one anecdote before someone else had one of their own.

Lillie considered herself a simple woman, living a simple life within her means, but telling these stories empowered her, making her more interesting, she thought. It gave her great pleasure to begin the meal with a narrative, and as she considered all the accounts she had shared over the years, she began to wonder if tonight she would share the one of the beautiful porcelain dish that came all the way from Greece in which to serve her mother's famous glazed carrots.

Chapter 11

A half-hour earlier, Joan found herself well-rested from an afternoon of napping on the front porch. She sat in the sun, listening to the leaves fall softly from the towering and colorful trees. With her sweater draped around her shoulders and her glasses resting on her nose, she had fallen asleep while journaling. She awoke to the mixed aromas swirling through the air, and she became keenly aware that she was hungry and couldn't wait to eat. She lifted her wrist toward her face and positioned her head so she could see the time through her bifocal and noticed that it was almost half-past five. She quickly gathered her things, stood up from the rocking chair, re-entered the inn, and headed up the stairs to her room. The front porch was now empty of visitors. The breeze continued to blow, and Joan's rocking chair continued to rock.

From the kitchen, Lillie heard the porch screen door open and close, and she was reminded that she needed to get the WD-40 out of the utility cabinet, but that thought came and went as she refocused her attention on the final details of dinner and setting the table.

It wasn't long before Lillie heard the six gongs on the beautiful grandfather clock that stood tall and distinguished in the foyer. She knew her guests would be arriving at any moment. Dr. Vic walked onto the second floor landing at the exact moment Joan walked out of her room on the same floor. Joan greeted Dr. Vic with her usual hardy "Hello!" and he responded with his not-so-usual greeting, a vigorous "Hello to you!" surprising even himself. He reached out his right arm in real traditional, gentlemanly fashion, and without hesitation, Joan slipped her arm into his, and the two descended to the main level of the inn.

Lillie couldn't help but notice the two arrived in the dining room together, causing her to wonder just how long they had been together today. The corners of her sweet lips curled up as she greeted her first two guests. Dr. Vic, again in a gentlemanly fashion, pulled a chair out for Joan, who was delighted that he chose the chair next to her for himself.

"Oh my!" Joan exclaimed, "the table is lovely. I knew it would be, but this exceeds my expectations!" Her eyes scanned across the table, noticing the perfect details that were intended to be the beginning of a perfect evening.

Simple arrangements of fresh flowers from Lillie's garden surrounded by unscented votive candles, were placed at each end of the table, leaving the exact center available for placement of the main course. While the table was designed to comfortably accommodate a party of eight, it was set for seven, and each setting included a dinner plate, salad plate, and bread plate. There were two forks to the left of the dinner plate, a dinner knife, steak knife and spoon to the right and both a dessert spoon and fork at the top of the plate. A glass of water was placed at each setting along with a sequence of four empty wine glasses lined up near the dessert spoon. A decorative napkin stood regally atop the salad plate. Joan reached for hers and placed it on her lap as Maddie and Michael walked into the room.

"Well, good evening," Joan welcomed, as if she were the official greeter of the gathering.

"Good evening!" Michael responded in his boisterous way.

Maddie added a gentle "Hello."

Michael wanted to sit next to Maddie for dinner, and while he may not have yet realized it, he appeared to be taking care of her. He pulled out the chair across from Joan for Maddie, and she took a seat. Michael sat next to her and across from Dr. Vic. Joan noticed how well rested they both looked.

Lillie entered the dining room from the kitchen and welcomed her quests with a bottle of Sauvignon Blanc, explaining that this particular wine from New Zealand pairs well with the light citrus salad topped with Feta cheese and pine nuts that she would soon present. Joan asked if they should wait for Amy and Drew, and just that quickly, they entered the room.

"Just in time!" Joan exclaimed. "We didn't want to start without you!"

Amy and Drew thanked them and took the two seats at the far end of the table.

Lillie poured Michael the first taste of wine. He gently swirled his glass, sniffed with a discerning nose and nodded with approval before he took a sip, which he swished in his mouth for a moment before swallowing. He smiled at Lillie, and she poured for the others, including herself. She then lifted her glass and toasted in gratitude to her guests for staying at her bed and breakfast and for the wonderful friendships she had developed with them all. Glasses clinked to accompanying "here-here" as the evening festivities began. Lillie the presented each guest with a tempting citrus salad. No one realized that Amy did not drink her wine.

A basket filled with a variety of breads was passed around as everyone enjoyed the salads. Conversation picked up as guests shared with one another the events of their day, and Lillie was delighted by the sounds of happy laughter filling the room, a strong indication she would not likely need to tell a tale this evening.

The bottle of Sauvignon Blanc was emptied, as were the salad plates, which Lillie removed and delivered to the kitchen. She returned with a bottle of pinot noir. Once again Michael not only approved the wine, but he also made a toast. He held his glass up toward Lillie.

"To Lillie," he announced, "hostess supreme and the best innkeeper in Louisville!"

"To Lillie!" all agreed, followed by more clinking of glasses.

Lillie thanked her guests with a slight curtsy and disappeared into the kitchen while conversation continued. She returned with a tureen of beef and barley soup that she explained would pair well with the pinot noir. She served each guest individually before sitting down to enjoy her own. When finished, she disappeared once again into the kitchen to make final preparations before serving the main course, which required a different wine selection, a French Syrah that she quietly poured for her guests. By this time, tasting for approval was unnecessary.

She placed a serving bowl at one corner of the table and another at the opposite corner. Between the Sauvignon Blanc and the pinot noir, the guests were enjoying themselves so much they barely discerned when Lillie removed their soup bowls.

Finally, Lillie entered the dining room with the main course. The roast was cooked to perfection, sliced for serving, and delivered to the center of the table, bringing a halt to all conversation. Lillie had the attention of her guests as she described the meal of Top Sirloin with a spicy rub, shiitake mushroom risotto, and (as she waved her hand toward the serving bowl at the far end of the table) gourmet cooked glazed carrots. "Please help yourselves, y'all," Lillie announced, and she took her seat.

By this time, Amy now had three glasses of wine at her place setting that she was not drinking, and she didn't know how she was going to avoid telling everyone about her pregnancy if they noticed. The others were enjoying their wine immensely, including Drew. It occurred to Amy that it was very possible no one would even notice she wasn't drinking. She wanted their special moment to be private and personal. She also wanted Drew to be coherent, and it was beginning to look like her plan may not work.

The meat platter made its way around the table, as did the risotto and carrots. Conversation turned to "mmmm's" and "ahhhhs," and once again, Lillie's culinary skills were a success. Having eaten at some of the most elite and interesting places in the world, Michael declared that this meal had been his favorite thus far, and Maddie smiled at Michael as she became increasingly enamored by his thoughtfulness. Joan expressed her gratitude for both the wonderful meal and fabulous company. An odd feeling came over Dr. Vic as he laughed and engaged with the others, and he felt happy—yes, very happy!

Everyone was deep in conversation. Michael told about a couple of his traveling experiences in Europe and Asia. Joan shared some child-rearing stories, like when her son ran away from home when he was six years old but only went as far as the end of the block because he knew he wasn't allowed to cross the street, and she laughed at the sweet memory. Dr. Vic talked about some of the good old days of being a doctor, before insurance companies and the government decided to take over, and both Maddie and Drew spoke of their work, Maddie as a financial analyst and Drew as a national sales director for an electronics company. Amy was unusually quiet, as if she were preoccupied, and of course she was.

Lillie spotted a couple of empty wine glasses, which she attentively replenished with another bottle of Syrah—except for Amy's.

"I hope y'all saved room for dessert," Lillie said, as she poured the wine.

"Oh my!" Joan exclaimed, "I will need a few minutes for all this delicious food to settle, but I would never turn down dessert." Lillie smiled.

Guests continued to sip their wine and enjoy conversation as Lillie cleared the table. She was pleased when she saw that most of the food had been devoured. The apple pies had cooled long before now, so she warmed them up a few minutes before topping with ice cream and serving. Although it seemed that most of her guests had adequately imbibed, she opened a bottle of Italian Muscat to pair with the apple pie. It was unanimous that this was a grand finale to a perfect meal.

The conversation diminished considerably while everyone feasted on the apple pie a la mode. Suddenly Drew noticed that Amy had four full glasses of wine sitting in front of her.

"Waste not, want not," Drew remarked as he reached across Amy, took the glass of Syrah as if it belonged to him, and continued imbibing.

Amy didn't mind sharing her wine, but her concern was growing as Drew's drinking was now more than adequate. Her plans of a quiet, joyous celebration with her husband were dissipating as she watched Drew get sloppy with his alcohol. She had never seen him like this before, but she had no idea of the heavy burden he was carrying or how concerned he was as he anticipated the next conversation he knew he would have with his wife.

Others also noticed Drew was drinking more and Amy was not drinking at all. Joan sensed something was going on with the couple who seemed so in love when she met them this morning at breakfast, but who also were visibly preoccupied. Earlier today she thought it was her maternal instincts, and indeed it may have been, and it may be those same instincts now that inspired Joan to engage Amy in conversation.

"Amy, you look lovely tonight," Joan remarked.

"Well, thank you, Joan…as do you."

Drew looked at Joan, then Amy, and added, "Amy always looks lovely…always, always, always…she is perfect in every way."

Amy blushed, but this time it was because she was becoming embarrassed for Drew, and she patted him on the leg as if to say *enough*. Drew was clueless as he reached across Amy once again and retrieved her glass of pinot noir.

"Ahhhhh, so good. Amy, I have no idea why you are willing to waste such excellent wine."

Amy didn't even know how to respond, so she just smiled.

Dr. Vic had been enjoying his wine too, and being the knowledgeable physician that he was, and in an effort to fully participate in the conversation, he shared his own hypothesis.

"Well, drinking is not recommended for women who are expecting," which he said as if it were the most natural and acceptable response.

Already at a loss for words, Amy froze, as did the intuitive Joan. Michael and Maddie were politely quiet as they finished their apple pie. Lillie started clearing the table and retreated into the kitchen.

"What?" Dr. Vic asked, "you never heard that?" and he indulged in another bite of apple pie.

It took a minute, but Drew suddenly realized what was said and he reached across Amy again for another glass of her wine, which he drank in its entirety, returning the empty glass to the table. He looked at Amy, who by this time appeared a bit blurry to him.

"Oh, Drew!" Amy exclaimed, "I have wanted to tell you but I've been waiting for the right moment—a private moment with just the two of us," and she glared at Dr. Vic. "I was hoping that would be tonight, just a little later…when we returned to our room and were alone. But YES, Drew, I am pregnant! I just found out earlier this week. I'm so excited!" She threw her arms around Drew's neck. Everyone applauded.

Drew was motionless. Amy let go of him and pushed herself away so she could see his face, which she noticed had not changed from his original shocked response.

Drew started to babble some jibber-jabber that could not be understood.

"What, Drew? What?" Amy begged.

Drew composed himself the best he could under the circumstances, cleared his throat and said in somewhat of a slurred fashion, "Amy, I had something very important to tell you, too, and I have also been looking for the right time and place. I have been a nervous wreck trying to find the words to tell you what my doctor told me earlier this week; I'm sterile. Sterile, Amy! I cannot father any children. I was terrified to tell you because I know how much it means to you to have children. I can't father children, Amy! So, who did? Who is the father of your child?"

Dr. Vic spat out the sip of Muscat he was swirling in his mouth. Lillie picked up a few more empty plates and returned to the kitchen. Maddie and Michael sat silently as Michael reached over and held Maddie's hand—again. Joan's mind was processing what she had just seen and heard. She immediately recalled the lovely and romantic couple with whom she had breakfast earlier today, and she simply could not imagine that Amy had been unfaithful to her husband. Rarely at a loss for words, Joan did not know what to say.

"I'm so sorry, everyone," Amy said. "There has been a terrible misunderstanding. Drew, let's go to our room to have this discussion."

Drew hesitated, partly because he was in shock, partly because he was inebriated, and partly because he was hurt and angry. "I don't think there is much room for discussion, Amy, but I am returning to our room...to pack." Drew pushed himself away from the table, stood up, steadied himself and headed for the stairs. Amy directed him toward the foyer and up the stairs, Drew stumbling all the way.

Joan broke the silence. "Oh my—those poor darlings."

Dr. Vic finished off the last of his Muscat. "Yep...this is not good...not good at all. On the other hand, this meal was fabulous beyond words!" He patted his belly.

Michael agreed. "Fabulous indeed, Lillie," and he invited Maddie to join him for another walk. She immediately jumped out of her seat as she accepted the opportunity.

Lillie poked her head around from the kitchen when she heard the front door close as Maddie and

Michael left, and she saw Joan and Dr. Vic remained sitting at the table.

"Is everything okay?" she asked.

"Well, that remains to be seen," Joan replied, "but I certainly hope so. They are such a lovely couple, but oh my—this is a serious predicament."

"That's an understatement," responded Dr. Vic, who then looked up at Lillie. "You have outdone yourself, young lady. This meal was the best."

Joan agreed as she got up and began helping clear the table, and once again, Lillie insisted that she go enjoy herself. Dr. Vic rose from his seat and invited Joan to have a cup of coffee on the porch. She accepted.

Alone in her thoughts, Lillie began a walk down memory lane, remembering how she fell in love with cooking in an attempt to please her father and to fix their relationship. As good as this meal was, it wasn't good enough to fix Amy and Drew. She felt so bad for them. She didn't want to believe that Amy had betrayed her husband, and she felt so sad for Drew having learned that he cannot father children. She knew how he must feel, since she, too, was unable to bear children.

Joan and Dr. Vic helped themselves to coffee and went to the porch to rock and relax. They sat next to each other under a clear sky and enjoyed the crisp air and chilly breeze that caused tree branches to sway as they continued to distribute their colorful leaves onto the yard. The half-moon dimly lit the otherwise dark night, and the sound of leaves being crushed under the rocking chairs was melodic. It was hard for Joan to believe that only eight hours ago she was sitting in the same chair having a wonderful conversation with Michael Roth. Now her thoughts were of Amy and Drew, and she held them in peaceful prayer. This was Joan's mode of operation. She prayed for peace for those involved in difficult situations, peaceful outcomes of those situations, and a knowing of what was hers to do in all situations.

Dr. Vic sipped on his coffee thinking of Amy and Drew, as well. He knew what he had been through as an unfaithful husband, and more importantly, he knew the pain it caused for so many others. He wondered how Amy could have an affair with another man, yet seem so in love with her husband. He noticed how attentive they were to each other, and in particular Amy's interaction with Drew. *She just didn't seem the type*, he thought. He considered himself an authority on the subject. Curiosity was getting the best of him as his brain continued to examine the circumstances, and the scientist in him began deciphering the details. He started to believe there was a good explanation.

Chapter 12

Drew staggered into 2-A with Amy right behind him making sure he made it in one piece. Inebriation coupled with anger equaled potential danger, which Amy was smart enough to recognize. She could not believe the outcome of what was to have been a beautifully planned weekend filled with expectations of joy and celebration. *What the hell happened*, she wondered.

Like most who have over-indulged on great wine, Drew was unaware of his current limitations. He stumbled to the closest, threw open the door, and reached for his suitcase. He grabbed the handle and yanked the luggage, and as he pulled on the handle, the luggage got stuck amongst other items. He pulled and pulled until the handle came loose from the suitcase, the force of which threw Drew backwards and onto his ass. Now he was really pissed.

Amy came to his rescue, but Drew held up his arm as if to protect himself from her. He thrust his arm to push her away with enough strength that she ended up on her ass, too. Amy was a tiny woman with very little padding to protect her fall. Her saving grace was that she was sober, which allowed her to gain some control before she hit the floor. She was able to get up easily and check for bruises, which at this time, had not yet developed. She decided to leave well-enough alone and sat in the cushioned chair in the room while she watched Drew's drunken state unfold in slow-motion.

Amy and Drew had never had a physical confrontation in the past, and Amy could not believe they were having one now. Drew, on the other hand, thought he was responding relatively well to the news that his wife had been sleeping around and now was pregnant with another man's baby. He wondered how she could betray him. How long had this been going on? How many lies has she told? His head was spinning with wild imaginings before he mumbled some nonsense until his voice faded and his head rolled to one side…lying there on the floor in the exact place he fell…it was *lights out.*

Once it was clear that Drew was out for the night, Amy took a pillow from the bed and carefully placed it under his head. She removed his shoes before covering him with a blanket, and she sat there with him on the floor. She stroked his handsome face before leaning in to kiss his cheek. "I do love you, Andrew Stout," she said before she got up and readied herself for bed. She hoped she would be able to sleep after all of this.

Chapter 13

Maddie and Michael walked up St. James Court to and around Central Park and back down the other side of St. James Court. The homes were lovely and well preserved.

Before turning onto Belgravia Court, they stopped and admired The Pink Palace. A beautiful home built in 1891 as a gentleman's club and casino, it has had several owners since. The reason it is referred to as The Pink Palace was obvious, and it is a well-known landmark in this historic section of Old Louisville.

"I have heard some pretty fabulous parties have taken place in this famous pink mansion," Michael said, as they walked around the palace and admired its architecture and beautiful gardens.

"All of these homes are so beautiful with their towering frames, welcoming front porches, and immaculate gardens," Maddie commented. "These homes remind me of the town where I grew up in West Virginia, with rich history and great character. I can only imagine the stories that could be told."

"Speaking of stories," Michael said, "I wonder if things have calmed down at the inn. Poor Drew and Amy. What a mess they have to work through." They finished their walk and returned to Lillie's place. Joan and Dr. Vic were still sitting on the porch, both having finished their coffee and both still considering the events of this evening.

"Hello," Maddie said quietly, "may we join you?"

"Of course!" responded Joan, who always enjoyed company. Maddie and Michael took a seat.

"What a lovely evening," Michael opined, and the four engaged in casual conversation.

Chapter 14

Lillie was still in the kitchen. Preparing such a big meal for her guests was work she loved, but it required lots of clean-up. She scraped the dishes, scoured the pots, and filled the dishwasher with the first load, then continued to clean and prepare for the second. This size meal required a number of kitchenware items and utensils, but Lillie smiled while she worked. As a young girl, she learned to prepare her meals with love. She decorated with love, she laundered the sheets with love, and she even scoured the bathrooms with love as she cleaned after her guests' departure and prepared for the following visitors. Lillie may not have felt loved by her father, but because of him, she learned to love and appreciate others.

Lillie's mind wandered as she carried on with her work, and she often thought of her mother, who was the strongest woman she had ever known. She still pondered how her mom lived so many years with an angry and violent husband, and she cringed at the thought of how much she suffered. Growing up under those circumstances made Lillie weary of men and their intentions, but when she met Ben in high school, she let down her guard and fell in love.

Ben and Lillie were both eighteen years old and in their senior year of high school when they first met. In the second semester, Ben joined the Army, and he was to head to basic training in June following graduation. Before he left, he asked Lillie to marry him. Completely enamored, Lillie said yes. She longed to get out from under her parents' unhappy marriage and begin a happy marriage of her own, and sadly, her mother understood. Following graduation, she and Ben went to the Meade County Clerk's office and acquired their marriage license before Ben headed to Fort Knox for training.

In the meantime, Lillie and her mother planned the wedding, which took place following Ben's graduation from basic training. It was a wonderful memory for both Lillie and her mother. It would be the only wedding they would plan together, and they loved each other so much that it seemed it was an event for the two of them more than for Lillie and Ben. Ben was happy for Lillie and her mother to make all of the arrangements, as he didn't have time, and he knew how much it would mean to them.

With only a few days between basic training and his first assignment, they married in a small, quiet ceremony on the grounds of the Doe Run Inn in Brandenburg, Kentucky. Lillie wore her mother's wedding dress with a few alterations that her mother made, and Ben wore his uniform. Flowers were freshly picked from the garden the day before the wedding. Chairs were made available by the inn and were arranged close to the creek, which made an extraordinary setting for a wedding. The weather could not have been more perfect. The flow of the creek provided the music with the exception of a solo by a longtime family friend who sang Elvis Presley's "I Can't Help Falling In Love with

You." Lillie's father walked her down the aisle made of pink and red rose petals, and following the small reception, also on the grounds of the inn, Lillie and Ben offered their gratitude to the attendees and retreated to their room where they spent their wedding night.

Lillie loved to relive that night over and over in her memory. Ben was her first love and her first love-making experience. He had little familiarity himself, so the two of them were guided by their hearts. Knowing almost nothing at all, they were both scared; Lillie was completely terrified, as she had never seen a naked man before. Ben had made her feel calm, special, and comfortable. It was like dancing. Ben took the lead while Lillie followed, and together they waltzed through the most amazing experience of their lives.

Before she knew it, the kitchen was clean, and Lillie headed for the porch to see if her guests needed anything. She was happy to see Joan, Dr. Vic, Maddie and Michael all enjoying themselves.

"Hello," she said softly, "how are y'all doing? Does anyone need anything?"

"Thank you for asking, Lillie, but you have done enough; if we need anything, we can help ourselves.

Please sit and relax with us," Joan suggested, and Lillie took a seat.

Maddie mentioned their walk up and down St. James Court and around Central Park.

"There is so much history here," she acknowledged, "and Michael and I are most intrigued with *The Pink Palace*."

"Oh, yes," responded Lillie "there are some great stories to be told about that fabulous place. You know, it started as a gentleman's club and casino, and some stories are likely true but cannot be proven, if you know what I mean," she said with a wink. "Yes, it was a man's world; a private world, and what happened at The Pink Palace was to have stayed at The Pink Palace, which is why I don't believe all of the stories, realizing that many have been embellished to beyond believable," Lillie remarked.

"Today, though, there are still some great stories that come out of that mansion and whether they are true or not, they are fun to hear and share. Truth is, there isn't a home on this court that doesn't have a good story or two. It is a fabulous neighborhood, and the residents are friendly and love to have a good time. In fact, there are a couple of good stories that have been borne out of my own place, right here on Belgravia Court." Lillie smiled. "I expect by the end of this weekend, I will have yet another," she said, and she winked again.

"Tell us a story, Lillie…about this bed and breakfast," Maddie requested, and Lillie complied.

"Well, there haven't been many since I bought this house, but there was this lovely couple who spent the weekend here a few years ago in 3-B. They were sweet, in their late seventies, and had recently married—of course not for the first time. It is one of those wonderful accounts of teenage lovers who graduated from high school and went their separate ways. They married other people, had children and careers and at some point, their spouses died. Years later, the couple attended a high school reunion, reacquainted, and eventually married each other.

"They went to their room on a Saturday night, and when they didn't show up for Sunday breakfast, I assumed they were still reacquainting," she teased. "By noon, I had not seen or heard them and I became increasingly concerned. At 1 o'clock that afternoon, I ventured up the stairs to 3-B and tapped on the door, but no answer, so I knocked again—and again, no answer.

One more time, a little harder, I knocked, and when there was no answer this time, I used my master key to enter the room. It was still dark and quiet, and I whispered their names, but no response. I called their names louder, and still no response, so I turned on a light and was shocked to see them both lying there in bed. I was embarrassed, but I didn't know what else to do. I tiptoed closer to the bed and noticed no movement. The closer I got to them, the more curious and concerned I became, and when I approached the bed, I saw they were both dead! I was stunned!

"I can't imagine what I must have looked like. I started shaking and mumbling some nonsense, and then I realized I was alone, since all the other guests had checked out, but then I wondered if I really was alone. I had no idea what had happened: how did they die? Was it murder, or what? Maybe I was not alone after all, and the murderer may still be in this room or somewhere in the house! I became terrified!" Lillie became more animated as she retold the story with her arms flailing, and she continued with everyone's quiet attention.

"I tiptoed back out of the room, down the stairs, and out the door, which slammed behind me. If someone was in the house, they probably now realized I had left. I ran directly to my next-door neighbors' and thank God they were home! It was hard to make sense, but finally the neighbors calmed me down, followed by a call to the police, who arrived very quickly. They searched the house, which took forever, and returned to the neighbors to let me know there was no sign of an intruder. They asked me a bunch of questions about the couple, but I had known them only for the weekend, so I knew very little except that they were so sweet and so much in love. They were affectionate and thoughtful and seemed to really enjoy each other's company.

"The police explained that an investigation would begin, and of course I understood; however, this was both my home and my business, so I asked about what to expect, and they rambled off some process. They told me I could return to the house, but to stay out of room 3-B, which was just fine with me. Soon detectives were swarming all around, and I was like a gnat that occasionally got in their way."

"What happened, for heaven's sake?" Maddie demanded.

"Well," Lillie continued in a whisper so as to evoke a bit of intrigue, "at first glance, it looked like a murder/suicide or a double suicide, but after the investigation it was determined that Evelyn had died in her sleep, and when Robert woke and found her dead, he apparently felt he could not live without her, so he wrote a note that explained he had been widowed once before and didn't want to be a widower again. He said he loved both of his wives but surviving the death of his first wife was painful enough, and he couldn't do it again, so he swallowed what was left of some prescription medicine. If I had checked on him sooner, he might have lived, but there was no sign of life when I entered their room that afternoon."

The coroner removed the bodies and took them to the morgue, where they were identified by their children who had been called by the police. I met the children when they came to the inn to collect their parents' items. They were sad that their parents were gone, but they were grateful they had found each other and spent their final days together. They said that there had been an autopsy, and Evelyn died in her sleep of a stroke, and Robert died of an overdose of prescription sleeping pills that he had been given when diagnosed with sleep anxiety. There was no foul play."

"Oh my!" Joan expressed. "That poor, dear man." She sighed. "That poor couple!"

"So that was in 3-B, right? Between Michael's room and mine…right?" Maddie asked.

"Right," Lillie responded.

"You know, Lillie, Michael and I have both heard noises coming from that room…like someone coming or going or moving around in there," Maddie reported.

"I've heard that before, when other guests have stayed here, but I think it's just because the house is old," Lillie explained.

There was silence. It was getting late and everyone was a little sluggish from the big meal.

"I can't stop thinking of Amy and Drew. I hope everything will be okay with them," Maddie said. The loss of her brother was devastating, but she was beginning to realize that everyone has personal challenges, and they are all relative on the pain scale. Now, in just twenty-four hours, she has met and fallen for a man, and she couldn't remember the last time she felt this alive.

She blamed herself for the loss of her brother, and she never could find the pathway to forgiveness. Now she is here with a couple whose greatest dreams were about to be fulfilled when circumstances got in the way. Maddie envisioned having children one day, and her mind began to wander as she considered the possibility. *Michael would make a good father*, she thought. *He is strong, secure, worldly, and successful. Had he ever considered having kids?*

Joan recalled for a moment of how dreadful it felt when she learned that her second husband had betrayed her and their marriage vows. She knew it was an experience not easy to forgive and impossible to forget, and she quietly sent up a silent prayer of peace for both Amy and Drew.

The usually quiet Dr. Vic piped up. "This could all be a horrible misunderstanding, you know. These things happen more often than anyone would like to think, but mistakes do occur in the world of medicine, and particularly in this area of specialty. Has it occurred to anyone that maybe Amy has not betrayed her husband,

and maybe…just maybe, Drew's physician made a mistake, or the lab miscalculated the results of his fertility test or got them mixed up with someone else's results?"

"That would be the best news," Joan responded.

"I think it is more than remotely possible," Dr. Vic responded. "I need to speak with Drew, but first he needs to sober up. He was in a pretty bad way after dinner, between a full belly, way too much wine, and the thought of having been betrayed by his beloved—well, my guess is he will have to overcome one giant headache before anyone can make much sense to him. Maybe I can talk with Amy." He turned to Joan and said, "I expect we could use your help," to which Joan was more than happy to oblige.

Michael had been rocking back and forth, listening to the conversation but not really participating. He had little experience in things such as those being discussed, but he found it very interesting just the same. It had become quiet again for a moment, and Michael yawned.

"I beg your pardon. It appears to be my bedtime," he said as he stood up and stretched. "Maddie…may I walk you to your room?" he asked, and Maddie nodded.

"Goodnight, folks. I'll see you at breakfast," Maddie promised, and she and Michael walked into the inn, catching the screen door to keep it from slamming.

"Well, believe it or not, I have a few things to prepare for breakfast," Lillie reported as she stood from her chair.

"Oh, you poor dear. May I please help you?" Joan asked.

"Absolutely not," Lillie responded. "I don't have that much to do. I'll see you in the morning."

"Thanks for a lovely meal, Lillie," Joan said, and Lillie smiled as she departed.

It was just Joan and Dr. Vic sitting on the porch now. The breeze, still gentle and warm, coupled with the sound of wrestling leaves came together like soft music.

"You are a wise woman, Joan," Dr. Vic said. "You offer good insight and advice, and you are patient and without judgment—very good qualities that I assume developed from some of your own life experiences."

"Yes, indeed," Joan said as she belted out a hardy laugh. "So, Victor, what's our plan for Amy and Drew?" she asked.

"Well," he responded, "let's see what happens at breakfast. First, we'll see if they show up. If they do, we can make small talk among ourselves, which will inevitably lead to tonight's dinner conversation." He looked sheepishly at Joan, and with a wink of his eye, he drew his right hand toward his mouth to mischievously twist the end of his imaginary handlebar mustache.

"Aha," Joan responded. "And if they don't show up at breakfast?"

"Well, this will definitely require a plan. Let's see, if they don't show up, you can go to their room and knock on the door, hoping Amy will answer. If she does, you can invite her to meet with you…and entice her by telling her there may be a medical explanation. By her response, you should know right away if Amy is telling the truth about her fidelity."

"How so?" Joan inquired.

"If Amy is ambivalent, she is probably not telling the truth, but if she is open to discussion, then she probably is telling the truth and anxious for some explanation that will bring a peaceful and happy resolution to their situation."

"So, we need a plan C, right? If Amy is not telling the truth—if she is pregnant with another man's baby—what then?"

"We strongly encourage the truth, Joan," Dr. Vic responded. "The sooner the truth is told, the better. Believe me—been there, done that. One lie leads to another, then another, until many people are involved and hurt. If Amy is having an affair, she needs to confess."

"Well…there is only so much anyone can do, but I am certainly willing to do what I can to help. I'm in." She raised her hand toward Dr. Vic's for a high-five, to which he reciprocated. "Best we get some sleep."

"You know, I'm not used to getting up early when I'm here. Would you mind knocking on my door before you head for breakfast?" asked Dr. Vic.

"Of course. Good night." Joan headed for her room.

Dr. Vic sat on the porch by himself for a few minutes before Lillie appeared at the front door.

"I'm turning in, Dr. Vic. Anything you need before I do so?"

"Not a thing," Dr. Vic responded. "Get some rest: you deserve it. Thanks for a wonderful meal. I plan to be at breakfast, so I can see what all the fuss is about." He smiled. "I'll lock up."

Lillie smiled back while thinking how Dr. Vic appeared to be mellowing, and she appreciated his blossoming demeanor. "Thank you. See you at breakfast."

Dr. Vic knew if he didn't get to bed himself, he would likely wake up in the morning on the porch. He entered the foyer without noticing that one of the neighborhood cats had managed to sneak in at his feet. He quietly closed and locked the screen door, and then he closed, locked and bolted the front door. He stood in the foyer for a moment and admired the structure and décor of the inn. The ambiance was like a cozy home filled with love, and he thought to himself how perfect it is that no matter what may happen throughout the course of a day, there is much comfort in finding oneself safe at home knowing that tomorrow holds promise.

He, too, recognized his own mellow moment and wondered if he was finally learning from his own mistakes. *I can't change my past*, he thought to himself, *but maybe I can change my future*. He headed up the stairs, and as he walked past Drew and Amy's room, the floor creaked. He stopped—there was no noise coming from their room, and the floor creaked some more as he continued to his room, closing the door quietly behind him.

Chapter 15

Amy was still awake, lying in bed alone. Her head was filled with thoughts coming and going. She was sad and disappointed . . . she could never have imagined this moment in her life, and now she was sick with fear and frustration. Drew had never been this drunk, not even in his college days, and Amy was certain she would have to literally drag him out of the inn tomorrow. What a sight she had created in her imagination. This had been one of the longest days of her life and she just wanted it to be over. She prayed she could get some sleep.

Joan was sitting in her room, dressed in her nightgown, robe and slippers, while sipping on hot tea. With pen in hand, she opened her journal and supposed she might be up all-night writing about the events of this day. It was in her journaling, though, that answers came to her, and she hoped that her mind would be illumined with some wisdom that would guide her to knowing what is hers to do regarding Amy and Drew, though she realized that maybe there was nothing for her to do.

Joan began her journaling with *We live and learn.* Her writing became prolific as she wrote and sipped tea before noticing how quickly an hour had passed. She closed her eyes and asked the universe if it was finished, and when nothing new came to her, she closed her journal, put down her pen, and climbed into bed under the fluffy covers that enveloped her as she relaxed and invited a good night's sleep. Her last thoughts were of gratitude for all of her blessings.

Lillie heard Dr. Vic come in, so after a few minutes, she got up and walked around all the rooms on the main level of the inn and secured the doors. She had already checked the back yard and gate, but she felt compelled to check the front door to assure it was secure as Dr. Vic had promised, and it was. She smiled at herself and her tendency to be just a little obsessive, and she headed back to her room. She stopped dead in her tracks when she heard a noise…then nothing…so she felt safe to return to her room. The old inn had many noises, and she thought of how the house had aged, just as she had.

Like the other rooms, hers was warm and cozy. It smelled of lavender and looked like a picture in a magazine. She had a window that opened to the back yard where she could sit and enjoy the garden from inside. The garden was filled with wildflowers, which were now starting to lose some of their blooms, and the beautiful green foliage was beginning to transition into the lovely colors of autumn.

This late at night, Lillie couldn't see her garden, but she appreciated knowing it would be lovely when she awakened in the morning. The window blinds were drawn, and she sat in her chair to remove her shoes. She disappeared into her bathroom to freshen up before crawling into bed and under the covers that were as comfortable and cozy as they looked. Lillie cherished her rest, particularly in the warm and fuzzy home that she fashioned. She had a great appreciation for what she had created because it was the exact opposite of the fear and discomfort of her upbringing. She felt safe now, and at peace.

She had a comfortable life and was doing what she loved, but Lillie often thought of her ex-husband and the life they might have had together. She wondered what she may have missed, having made such a quick decision to marry when she was just out of high school and so naïve. Her young husband was handsome and kind and thoughtful and not the slightest bit abusive. She didn't realize then how much more there was to a relationship, and unfortunately, neither did her new husband. Both Lillie's parents and Ben's were apprehensive about the two of them marrying so young, but at least Lillie's mother understood Lillie's longing for a loving relationship.

Ben left for basic training in late August as planned, and Lillie was alone after less than a week of marriage. She lived in a small apartment near her parents' home. She and Ben wrote love letters to each other almost every other day, and she anxiously anticipated the mail carrier's routine arrival. She saw her mother frequently but continued to avoid her father, even though he was aging and not able to be as physically abusive as he had been in the past. Lillie knew, however, that her father continued to mentally abuse her mother, the damage of which was often worse than the physical harm. She hoped her mother would put that miserable old man in his place, but she never did. Lillie didn't know if her mother was a saint or a fool, but she did know she loved her dearly and would do anything to protect her.

Lillie's memories returned to her wedding night so many years ago. Her eyes closed as she fell fast asleep. One could only hope that her dreams would take off where her wedding night memories ended.

Chapter 16

Earlier in the evening, Michael walked Maddie to her room. Maddie unlocked the door, walked through the threshold, and turned around to say good night. "I had such a wonderful evening, Michael…despite the Amy and Drew fiasco. The dinner was fabulous, the wine divine, and the company delightful—well, again, despite the Amy and Drew fiasco," she repeated.

Michael towered over Maddie's small and very fit frame, and he looked down at her beautiful facial expressions. "Wow—it is so good to see you smile," he remarked. Their eyes were locked. Michael moved his hand to behind Maddie's head to hold it while he leaned in to kiss her. It started as a small innocent kiss and grew into an intense and passionate romantic kiss as Maddie melted into Michael's arms. He drew her in closer. Without letting go, both managed to enter Maddie's room and close the door behind them. The moment was magical.

Maddie was weak with anxious anticipation as Michael picked her up and placed her on her bed. He whispered, "Are you ready, Maddie? I want to make love to you." Maddie reached her arms around Michael's neck to pull him in closer to her. "I'll take that as a yes," he said, and he sat at the side of her bed and kissed her again. When their lips parted, she took in a deep breath and exhaled with a sense of release. There was a quiet pause—giving Maddie an opportunity to excuse herself.

"I'll be right back, Michael. Don't go anywhere," she insisted, and she walked to the bathroom across the hall to freshen up.

This was the first time Michael wished he had his own bathroom, so he could freshen up too, but he was grateful at least that they were the only two on the third floor. He took advantage of Maddie's absence and went to his room to clean up the best he could. He apparently had forgotten that Maddie specifically told him not to go anywhere.

Maddie was gone only a few minutes before she returned to her room, and she was disappointed to find Michael absent. *Oh well*, she thought, *he is probably trying to be a gentleman and not take advantage of me*...even though she wanted him to. She turned down the covers of her bed, sat in her chair and removed her shoes and jewelry. She breathed a sigh of disappointment as she fell back into the chair, closed her eyes, and quivered as she relived the kiss of only moments ago.

Maddie was startled when she heard a soft knock at her door, and she was delighted when she opened it. "I thought you left me here all alone—but since you're back, can we pick up where we were?" she asked as she reached up and leaned in to kiss Michael with even more passion than before. Michael responded in kind. He picked her up again and placed her on the bed.

Maddie looked into his beautiful blue eyes. She stopped thinking altogether and was guided completely by her instincts. She wanted Michael on this night like nothing she had ever known, and she took his hands and guided them to her body.

Michael had already been admiring Maddie's svelte figure, and he was somewhat anxious as he began to disrobe her. He was not disappointed when his expectations were exceeded by her beauty, and he gently touched her warm, smooth skin. Maddie tingled all over, and a smile came upon her as she reached again for Michael's face and stroked it tenderly. She could see he was pleased and wanted her as much as she wanted him.

Maddie pulled Michael's shirt up and ran her hands over his back and down to his waist where she was forced by his belt to pause. Michael took over and removed his shirt, then his pants and finally his boxer shorts. Maddie was impressed with his muscular body, and she caressed his shoulders and stroked his arms with her fingertips as she moved her hands down and around his strong biceps and across his chest.

Maddie caressed his face and then moved her fingers like feathers down his chest to his thighs. She glanced up at Michael as if to ask permission to touch more of him. Michael took Maddie's hands into his and placed them on his penis, where she fondled him with innate prowess, and to which he responded with great enthusiasm. She yearned for more.

Michael leaned in and kissed Maddie, intoxicating her with his passion. Maddie wrapped her athletic legs around Michael's torso and facilitated a flip that placed her on top of him. He looked up at her with a grin. She reached for his hands and placed them on her plump breasts and erect nipples that longed to be touched.

Michael's tender touches evoked such pleasure for Maddie, she could wait no longer. She reached down for Michael's hard penis and gently eased it into her. Maddie was wet with expectation, and she was not disappointed. Michael thrust himself into her as she gyrated avidly, an activity that continued until they arrived at an exhilarating climax, leaving them both happy and exhausted. Their lovemaking was symphonic.

Maddie curled up in Michael's arms and he held her close as they cherished the moment. Michael noticed she was teary-eyed.

"What is it, Maddie?" Michael asked. "Are you okay?"

"I've never been better—never, ever, ever," Maddie responded as she smiled through her tears, and Michael pulled her in even closer.

Chapter 17

Sunday morning arrived all too soon. Lillie was already in the kitchen adding the finishing touches to breakfast, which was not very different from Saturday's. She set the table for six, hoping everyone would partake, and she thought of Amy and Drew and wondered how they did through the night.

Because of her worry and concern, Amy had gotten up several times through the night to see if Drew was breathing as he lay on the hard floor. Amy thought, *he may be alive, but when he comes to, he is probably going to wish he was dead. Too much of a good thing can be bad, and wine is almost never an exception.*

Amy decided to get up before Drew was awake. If she showered and packed before Drew woke up, at least they would be ready to go if things got out of hand. Amy had enough embarrassment for one weekend, and she didn't want to be humiliated at another meal. She made sure Drew was as comfortable as possible and started her shower.

It was still early. Lillie was up because she had work to do. Amy was up because she never went to sleep. Maddie and Michael had fallen asleep, each with happy smiles that remained on their faces all night.

Dr. Vic fell asleep on his bed, atop his covers with the table light on and a pair of reading glasses slipping off his nose. An open book was resting on his chest as if he had intended to close his eyes for only a moment. By now he had been sleeping for hours.

Joan was awake, sitting up in bed, and journaling. She cherished this morning ritual to which she attributed her clear thinking. Her writing was interrupted by thoughts of the Stout's as she grappled to imagine that Amy would betray Drew, or anyone for that matter. She seemed genuine, and while Joan considered herself an intuitive person, she realized she had made her mistakes, too. Still, it didn't seem possible. She completed her journaling, showered and prepared for her walk as she continued to process the situation and the possibilities, for which she prayed intently for a good outcome.

When he awoke, Dr. Vic began moaning and groaning as he fought the promise he made Joan to show up for breakfast. When he regained full consciousness, he was able to consider some good reasons to not attend including knowing that Joan would understand, or he rarely ate breakfast, or he was on retreat when he often slept through the morning. The excuses were plentiful, but he soon realized an opportunity to begin doing some things differently. He was familiar with the quote: "If you want something different, do something different," and with that thought in mind, he got up, shaved, showered and dressed.

He had an uncommon sense of optimism about him, and he liked the feeling of not dreading the day. After he dressed, he began gathering his things as he prepared for checkout early that afternoon. He thought of breakfast and how things would work out with the Stouts, which made him recall the mess he made of his own life, and he hoped there may be an opportunity for him to redeem himself somewhat by helping Amy and Drew.

Amy finished packing. She was showered, dressed and ready to go. She knelt down next to Drew. He was breathing but still relatively unconscious. Amy didn't know what to do with herself. She was nauseous and was unsure if it was morning sickness or if she was just so upset with the way things were going, and she decided it was a little of both. She took a deep breath, and suddenly felt worse. She ran into the bathroom just in the nick of time to vomit most of her dinner from last night. She flushed the toilet but stayed close just in case she wasn't finished, and within a few minutes the nausea subsided. She washed her face and brushed her teeth and felt much better, though she knew she could use some fresh air. It was early, so she wrote a quick note to Drew: *Went for a walk, be back soon. Love, Amy.* She grabbed her key and sweater, and quietly ventured down the stairs to the foyer. She opened and quietly closed the screen door, attempting to get out without being noticed.

They moved barely a muscle by morning. Maddie woke up to Michael watching her. "I think that smile stayed on your face all night," Michael said.

"I am happy, Michael!" she exclaimed. "I thought I had forgotten how to be happy, but you helped me remember. I feel like I couldn't stop smiling if I tried."

"The feeling is mutual," Michael responded.

"I prefer not to end this wonderful moment, but we better get ready for breakfast," Maddie said.

"Maybe we can get ready faster by taking one shower instead of two," Michael suggested.

"I like the way you think, Michael Roth." They got up and started to get ready.

Maddie heard a noise coming from the room next door again—the room that was supposed to be empty this weekend.

"Did you hear that?" she asked. Michael listened but didn't hear anything.

"Shhhh…" Maddie cautioned. "Please listen. Hear that?" she asked again.

"Yes, but that could be anything—or anyone. It could be Lillie getting ready for a new guest or the air ventilation system. In these older homes, it could be the ghosts of that couple Lillie told us about." Michael looked at Maddie and laughed.

"Yes—well, don't think that hasn't crossed my mind, but I suppose it is more likely to be the air ventilation system—or maybe nothing at all," Maddie replied.

"Now…about that shower," Michael reminded her.

Every day was new and exciting for Joan. She learned a long time ago to let go of expectations, other than to know it would be a perfect day, regardless of her location, or the weather, or worldly affairs, or current company. It was all perfect and opportunities were abundant. Her walk this morning was as lovely as yesterday morning's, and she wondered if it was possible that the leaves were even more colorful today. Maybe they were or maybe it was her sense of appreciation. Either way, Joan was in her usual state of optimism and gratitude, and she was happy.

Joan's awareness was directed to the figure of a person crossing the street ahead, and she recognized it was Amy. She wanted to shout her name, but it was early, the neighborhood was still very quiet, and she wasn't sure how Amy was doing this morning, so she decided to say nothing. She continued her walk, and as she got closer to the inn, she saw someone already sitting on the porch enjoying the morning.

"Good morning, Dr. Vic," she said. "I must admit that I was not certain you would make it for breakfast, but I was prepared to knock on your door in a few minutes."

"You know, I tried to come up with some excuses to miss it, but I thought better, and here I am! And by the way, Joan, please call me Vic," he insisted.

Will do, Vic," Joan responded as she took a seat in the rocking chair next to him. "Guess who I saw on my walk this morning?" Joan asked.

"I give up. Who?" he responded.

"Amy! She doesn't know I saw her, but I expect she will be returning soon. Are you prepared for a discussion this morning?" she asked.

"Well, I am prepared...I guess what matters is whether Amy is prepared...and Drew," he replied.

Joan looked at her watch, and it was just past 8 o'clock. "I think we have an hour until breakfast, and it smells like Lillie is in the kitchen."

"Yes, I saw her when I came downstairs. She was busy preparing food and the table had already been set. She is quite a gal."

"Indeed," Joan agreed.

Joan and Vic sat and rocked and made small talk. Vic was not much for conversation this early in the morning. Even on office days he didn't schedule his first patient until 9 o'clock. He knew he was more amicable after his coffee, which he would enjoy while reviewing medical records and returning phone calls. Workdays always started early and ended late for him, which is why he has such great appreciation for sleeping in, an occasion that was all too rare, and he pondered the idea of retiring sometime soon.

Lillie broke the silence as she walked onto the porch with a cup of tea for Joan and a cup of robust coffee for Dr. Vic.

"Ahhh…you must have been reading my mind," Dr. Vic commented with gratitude.

"And mine," added Joan. They were both quick to take the first sip. "You are an angel, Lillie," said Joan, and Dr. Vic agreed.

"Let me know if you need anything else. I'll be in the kitchen." Lillie said as she walked away.

Joan looked up from sipping her tea and saw Amy approaching. She nudged Vic, who also looked up. "Good morning, Amy," Joan greeted, and Vic echoed.

"Good morning," Amy responded. "Listen, I'm really sorry about dinner last night," she said. "I know I have a number of apologies to make, so I'm glad to see you and get started."

"Oh, Amy—you don't need to apologize. I'm sorry for you, you poor dear," Joan said. "I realize your plans for a private, happy moment fell apart in front of all of us, and I'm so sorry." Amy tried to wipe her tears before they were noticed.

"It's awful. I was so excited to share my news, and this IS Andrew's baby! I have no idea what he is talking about with this sterile thing. What in the world? I have never been unfaithful…oh my God! I'm mortified, and I don't know what to do! Drew is a mess, still plastered on the floor of our room—at least that is where he was when I left him. I didn't even know he was going to a doctor for this. We had already been through the infertility process, and we were actually talking about adopting. When I learned I was pregnant, I knew this would be the most wonderful and amazing news for Drew." She began to cry out loud.

"Amy, come and sit down. I think we might be able to help," Joan replied, and she looked at Vic as if to cue him. "Tell her, Vic," she insisted as she sat next to Amy, holding her hand.

"Well, Amy, I have been a doctor for a long time, and it is possible that either Drew's lab results were incorrect, or it could be that they were correct, but the two of you beat the odds. What did your infertility results find?" he asked.

Amy sniffled, and wiped her nose with the tissue Joan offered. "Well, they weren't really conclusive. We were told that everything was essentially fine, but that Andrew did have a low sperm count—low enough that it was recommended we could keep trying and never get pregnant, which was likely, or we could consider adopting. Because that is also a long and arduous process, we were encouraged to focus on the latter option. Drew didn't want to adopt; he has been angry that it was his fault that we may never have children, but I didn't realize he had given up altogether. He has been acting like something was wrong. He has been distant and deep in thought, but I had no idea why. Apparently he has seen yet another doctor who confirmed his sterility, so he is angry about that, and now he is angry because he also thinks I have been unfaithful!" She threw her hands over her face and started to cry again.

"Oh, Amy, everything will be okay. First, we have to get Drew off the floor of your room and get him sobered up so he can make sense of all this. Then we need to let him know that somewhere along the course of events, there has been some misinformation that can be explained, and if it comes to this, you can have a paternity test to prove that Drew is the father of your baby. I know this is not how you planned this event to unfold, but sometimes things happen for reasons we do not understand. This is not the end of the world, my dear. This is a new beginning in your lives." Joan's words were direct and thoughtful. Amy knew what she had to do, and she knew she didn't have to do it alone.

"We're here for you," Dr. Vic offered.

Amy wiped her tears, then gave both Joan and Dr. Vic big hugs. She looked at her watch, which showed it was 8:45, and she headed directly to her room.

Vic looked at Joan with approval. "You handled that very well. I am impressed."

"Why, thank you," she replied with her typical laugh. "I hope everything else goes as well."

Just then, Maddie and Michael came out onto the porch. Even though Joan and Vic had just met these new friends less than twenty-four hours ago, today it seemed they were meeting two completely different people.

"Good morning, you two!" Joan greeted, and Dr. Vic rose to shake Michael's hand.

"Good morning!" they both responded joyously. Maddie and Michael probably thought they looked just like they did yesterday, but they did not; they looked refreshed and rejuvenated, and Joan and Vic noticed.

"Hmmm," commented the usually quiet Dr. Vic. "Are you the same Maddie and Michael I met yesterday?"

"Well of course we are," Maddie responded. "Why do you ask?"

Dr. Vic just looked at her, and Maddie turned to Joan inquisitively.

"Oh, I agree. We are not seeing the same two people we met yesterday, Vic. I think you are correct.

These two who say they are Maddie and Michael are imposters. I'm certain!" Joan said, and she laughed.

"What?" Maddie asked. She looked at Michael and grinned sheepishly as the blush of embarrassment colored her face.

"Oh, you guys" Maddie responded blushingly. "I think we *are* different people today!" she said. Michael put his arm around Maddie.

"Okay, the secret is out. It is true—Maddie and I had a wonderful evening, and we are not ready for the weekend to end. Funny how life happens when you're not even looking," Michael commented. Quick to change the subject, he then asked, "Does anyone know how Amy and Drew are this morning?"

Dr. Vic responded, "Amy seems to be doing well; she's tired because she got little, if any, sleep, but we saw her here on the porch this morning, and I think she knows how to handle the situation—that is, assuming she is able to get Drew off the floor before checkout today."

Lillie summoned everyone to breakfast, and the porch group made their way into the dining room.

Chapter 18

Amy returned to her room and found that Drew did manage to pick himself up off the floor and find his way to the shower. She was grateful that she didn't have to literally pick him up. She viewed him through the glass shower door and was reminded of how much she adored him. She couldn't stand it that he would even consider for a second that she was unfaithful, especially at such a monumental moment in their lives together. She looked around the room to see what needed to be picked up and packed. Drew's clothes were thrown on a chair, and his shoes were still where Amy put them the night before.

Drew had picked up the pillow and blanket from the floor and placed them on the bed next to his suitcase that was partially packed. Drew must have been reasonably cognizant and was standing upright. Amy thought, *so far, so good*.

The water shut off in the shower, and shivers ran up and down Amy's back and arms as she anticipated his demeanor and the conversation she knew they had to have. They had fought very little in the past, and never over something so significant. She sat in the chair and waited patiently for Drew, who was toweling off.

He saw Amy's reflection in the mirror, and he remembered bits and pieces of the night before—how angry he was at her and how humiliated he had felt in front of everyone. He was still stunned and maybe still a little inebriated. He knew he had to talk with Amy, but he was hurt and somewhat unsure of his ability to have an intelligent conversation. *What will I do now*? he wondered. *Of course I have to get divorced. How could I stay married to a woman pregnant with another man's baby? What would our parents think? Our friends?* He wondered if the *baby-daddy* was one of his friends. The wild imaginings were running through his head like hallucinations from a bad acid trip. He rubbed the towel vigorously over his full head of hair as if it would rub out the torment. He looked up at Amy's reflection again, this time recalling how much he loved her and how, less than twenty-four-hours ago, he was fretting over how he would tell her that he would never be able to father any children. It meant so much to both of them, and he knew how terribly disappointed Amy would be. Now, everything is different...*it's all so wrong,* he thought, and he toweled his hair with greater vigor even though it was already dry.

Amy never knew Drew to spend this much time on his hair, and she concluded he was stalling. She decided to take the first step. She stood up and walked to the bathroom door. Drew looked into the mirror again and made eye contact with her.

"Drew, we need to talk...can you sit with me...? Please?" she pleaded.

"Give me a minute to get dressed," he answered, and Amy returned to the chair.

Drew had mellowed since the night before, but he was still hurting and confused. He knew this talk needed to happen sooner rather than later and shouldn't wait until they were on the road or at home. He got dressed, combed his hair and took a seat on the edge of the bed across from Amy. He was as handsome now as he had ever been, and she felt so bad for him.

"Drew," she said, "there has been a terrible misunderstanding."

Drew was fuming inside and it was all he could do to keep from opening his mouth with statements he knew he would regret later; he bit his tongue.

"This baby is your baby. I know you said the doctor confirmed you are sterile, but he is wrong." Amy knew she had to get all of that out quickly before Drew would interrupt.

"I could never be with another man: I love YOU, Andrew Stout. I have always loved you, and I love you today in the same way I loved you on our wedding night, only more intensely." Drew was listening…still biting his tongue, but maybe not quite so firmly. "Doctors make mistakes, Andrew. Labs do, too. Something like that has to have happened to explain this situation. Either that, or this is the miracle we longed for and despite the correct lab results, we beat the odds. You have to believe me Drew," she pleaded, "but if you don't, we can have a paternity test performed." Then Drew had to say something.

"If labs make mistakes, how can we ever be sure that this baby is mine?" he asked sarcastically.

"I guess that is one of the things that makes love so special, Andrew, because when you're in love the way we are in love, you have to trust in that love. You are right—paternity tests can have inaccurate results, too, but I love you deeply, and I know without any doubt whatsoever that this is your baby I am carrying." Amy got up from the chair and sat next to Drew on the bed. She took his hand into her two tiny hands and held them as she looked up at him.

"Drew—please look at me," Amy asked, and he turned his face toward hers. "I love you, and only you. I am carrying your baby—our baby—and I need you. This baby needs you. This baby is a gift to us both. We have been blessed in spite of what the doctors have said or lab results showed. Please accept this gift with me."

Drew looked at Amy and wanted to believe she was telling the truth...*but what if she isn't?* he thought. It felt terrible to him yesterday to think he had been betrayed, and he was now in fighting mode. *What will happen if I let down my guard?* he asked himself. The last thing he wanted was to be made a fool of again.

"Andrew, I understand this has been difficult for you, but all this has been only a twenty-four-hour misunderstanding—a blip in our eight years of marriage. This can go away when you are willing to let it go. It isn't even real—this is only a misunderstanding!" Amy proclaimed. She was desperate; she wanted this to be over NOW. "We have so much to look forward to, Andrew. Let's not waste another minute. Dammit Drew—I don't know what else to say! I'm begging you to stop holding me hostage to a lie you're telling yourself." Amy took a deep breath. It was unusual for her to become so frustrated. Drew had not seen this side of her, and he did want to believe her.

"You're right, Amy," Drew responded, "we do need to move forward." He hesitated as he gave his thoughts a chance to slow down. "It is interesting how the brain works…how all of this makes me feel. Bottom line is, I love you, too, and only you, and the thought of having a baby—oh my God—it *is* a miracle! We can talk about this more on our way home, but for now, I expect we should make a presence at breakfast so I can make some necessary apologies."

Amy was ecstatic as she threw her arms around Drew and kissed him all over his face. Andrew took Amy's face into his hands and leaned in to kiss her. In one fell swoop, happiness had returned to Amy and Drew, and together they left for breakfast.

Chapter 19

Everyone looked up when Amy and Drew entered the dining room together, fifteen-minutes late. The looks on their faces were fun to watch as they went from stunned, to curious, to happy and finally to laughing out loud without anyone saying a word.

"Sometimes, words really get in the way…right?" Drew blurted out, and everyone laughed some more.

"Sit—sit," Lillie commanded as she pulled out two chairs for Amy and Drew, and they accepted.

"This breakfast is as fabulous as yesterday's. Dig in," Joan insisted.

"Not before I apologize to you all about my behavior last night at dinner," Drew announced.

"Enough said," Dr. Vic responded. "No apology necessary. It was a fabulous meal, thanks to Lillie, and really, a very fun occasion."

"Well, I appreciate you wanting to make this easy for me, but I ate too much, drank too much, and emoted too much over what I now realize was a misunderstanding." Drew picked up his juice glass and motioned it toward his wife. "To Amy—the mother of MY baby, and the most beautiful woman in the world. To the good health of you both!" Everyone raised their glasses.

A couple walking past the bed and breakfast were distracted by the sounds of clanking glasses and laughter heard through the open window in the dining room. "Sounds like a very good time going on in there," one said to the other.

The breakfast was delicious, and Lillie had once again outdone herself. The eating frenzy continued, and the conversation was fun and interesting. Maddie and Michael spoke of their budding relationship and plans to meet again soon, somewhere between Richmond, West Virginia, and Michael's next assignment.

Drew's demeanor was completely opposite of last night, and Amy was increasingly animated since last night's burden had been lifted from her shoulders. She spoke of decorating the baby's room, morning sickness, and telling their family and friends their news. She thanked everyone for being such an important part of this event, even though her plans did not unfold as she had hoped. She and Andrew discussed the unknowns, such as whether they have a girl or boy, where he or she would go to school—even college! They promised to keep in touch with everyone as information developed.

Joan expressed gratitude for new friendships, delicious food, and a great time. Her bright smile and pleasant personality made her excellent company, and her sparkling spirit and jovial laugh made her popular and fun to be around.

Dr. Vic had become somewhat bitter in his later years, but he was beginning to mellow as he learned that some things just aren't worth a fight. He was a remarkable physician and patient advocate. With retirement not far down the road, he thought that maybe he would see what he needed to do to move it even closer so he might begin to travel more and meet more interesting people, like those he met this weekend. Maybe write a book or articles for medical journals. He was a quiet man, who by his own admission didn't talk much so as to avoid interrupting his thinking process.

Lillie was sitting among all of her guests and enjoying their company. This particular group was like family, and she was sorry to see them go, but she had other pressing matters on her mind that required her attention. If everyone checked out early, that would be perfect for her. She took the last sip of her coffee and sat back in her chair. The conversation diminished as everyone finished their meal.

Just that quick the tranquil moment was interrupted by what was later identified as a cat's blood-curdling screech.

"MEOWWWWWWWWWWWWWWWWWW!"

The *cat alarm* startled everyone at the table, and a series of priceless hidden-camera moments began in slow motion. The scene could easily have been the best video never recorded, and as if the screech weren't enough, suddenly the boisterous cat came galloping through the kitchen as if to mimic an old *Tom and Jerry* cartoon, rounding the corner on the tile floor, all four paws slipping and sliding as it tried to gain some traction. When it reached the dining room, it was headed straight for Lillie, who had impulsively pushed herself away from the table and stood up as if she were going to get the hell out of there! The cat was lunging directly toward her, but she stepped out of the way, and it jumped first on her chair, then directly onto the table.

"Oh my God!" Lillie screamed. Everyone screamed.

All the guests pushed themselves away from the table. Arms were flailing; people were tripping over each other. Maddie started to fall, and Michael caught her but then fell, himself. The cat was spastic, trying to maneuver itself over the table through jams and jellies, which spilled over as did coffee, tea, and juice. The cat stepped on almost every plate, pushing and shoving some onto the floor, where they broke into tiny pieces. That damn cat never knew where it was going before making it to the opposite end of the table; it was literally running scared, and since cats aren't deep thinkers, it just kept reacting to its fear and sailed off the edge of the table, heading for the foyer, thinking it had found a way out. The screen door was closed so securely, all the cat could do was launch itself onto the aluminum mesh where it remained…hanging on for dear life with all claws firmly trapped within the tiny holes in the screen. All efforts to free itself were to no avail.

Dr. Vic saw an opportunity and ran for the door, grabbed the cat on the back of its neck, pushed the screen door open, yanked the cat backwards and set it free. He walked back into the foyer, closed the door, and returned to the dining room.

Lillie was beside herself. "Oh my God! How did that cat even get in here?" she screamed. "I'm so, so sorry!" she professed to everyone.

Dr. Vic started laughing until he couldn't stand up anymore. Drew was making sure Amy was okay, Michael had managed to get up off of the floor and confirm that Maddie was okay, Joan was making sure Lillie was okay. It turned out that no one was hurt, short of a few scrapes, however, everything was in disarray. Pancake syrup was everywhere. The cat spread it from the table through the foyer and onto the screen, where a couple of bees had already captured its scent. Everyone soon regained their senses.

"Come on, Lillie, I'll help you take care of this," Joan proposed, and all the others agreed to do the same.

"Absolutely not," Lillie insisted. "Clearly y'all need to take care of yourselves, plus I know you have deadlines to meet, so this comes with my responsibilities, and I am happy to take care of it. Y'all go get cleaned up. Why, it is already ten-thirty!"

"I still have medical records to do before patients in the morning," Dr. Vic said as he vanished to the second floor.

Amy and Drew were just as anxious to get on the road, so they went to clean up, too. Maddie and Michael didn't want to leave at all, but they knew they had to.

Maddie had work in the morning, and Michael had to prepare for his next article, so they headed for their rooms, too, not just to pack, but to have a proper goodbye. Michael winked as he said, "Let's go get cleaned up Maddie," and they, too, retreated to their rooms for the last time.

Only Lillie and Joan remained in the dining room. "Are you okay, Lillie?" Joan asked.

"Yes…yes, thank you, I am. Just preoccupied with other things, and now this," she responded.

"I'm happy to help, dear."

"Oh no, Joan, you have done enough to help me, and it looks like you got the worst of the jam and jelly. You go get cleaned up, too." Joan acquiesced and went to her room.

Chapter 20

Lillie wanted to cry. She was so upset about the disorder. This was the stickiest mess she could remember; jams, jellies, syrup, and sugar were everywhere! No one realized it was Dr. Vic who let that cat in the house—not even Dr. Vic. It was an accident with no harm intended. Dr. Vic survived with the least amount of harm, so it wasn't long before he was ready to depart. He straightened up his room, gathered his things and headed for the front room. He wanted to say goodbye to the others before leaving, so he placed his luggage near the couch and exited to the porch.

It was another beautiful fall day in Louisville, and relaxing on the porch was almost intoxicating to this aging and tired physician, so he got comfortable.

Amy and Drew came down the stairs soon thereafter, carrying their luggage onto the porch where they were greeted by Dr. Vic.

"It was such a pleasure meeting you Dr. Vic, and we can't thank you enough for your professional opinion and good advice," Drew said, and Amy agreed, as she reached to give him a hug.

"You two will be just fine, and hey, here is my contact information. I hope you will keep me posted on developments." He handed Drew his card.

"You bet we will," Drew responded. "In fact, I want to keep everyone posted. Would you mind giving my cards to the others and have them contact me with their information?"

"Of course," Dr. Vic replied. "Have a safe journey home." He watched the Stouts walk down Belgravia toward St. James Court until they were out of sight, and he returned to his rocker. It wasn't long before Joan appeared on the porch.

"You just missed the Stouts, but here is their contact information," he said, handing a card to Joan. "They want us all to let them know how to be contacted when the baby arrives."

"Oh, I'm sorry I missed them, but I don't blame them for wanting to get on the road. Thanks for the card, and thanks for helping those kids out! It has been a pleasure meeting you." She took a seat next to Vic. "Has Maddie or Michael come down yet?"

"No. My guess is they will wait until the last minute."

"I'd like to say goodbye to them, as well. And Lillie? Have you seen her?"

"No, but I could hear her working in there. What destruction!"

"Poor thing. I hope she doesn't expect any more guests for a while."

Joan and Vic sat and chatted for a bit, discussing the events of the weekend, the new friends they had made, and their plans upon returning home. The hour sped by when they heard the grandfather clock gong indicating it was one o'clock.

"Oh my!" Joan exclaimed. "I can't believe the time! I really must go, Vic. Again, it was a pleasure meeting you." She offered a handshake, and he reciprocated.

"The pleasure is mine. Too bad for us we didn't meet each other about 40 years ago."

She belted out a hearty laugh. "You are so right, but at least we met each other now, and I'd like to think we will meet again someday. Here is my contact info," she said, and she handed him a card.

Having waited until the very last minute, Maddie and Michael walked out onto the porch. "Yay! I didn't think I was going to get to say goodbye," Joan said as she offered a hug first to Maddie, then to Michael. "It has been such a pleasure meeting you both and getting to know you. One never knows who they will meet at times such as this, and I am very happy that I was able to spend my weekend with all of you!"

"The feeling is mutual. Our lives are changed forever after this weekend, and in my wildest dreams, I could not have seen this coming," Michael said, looking over at Maddie with that magical twinkle in his eyes, and Maddie smiled back.

"You kids have a safe trip to wherever it is you are both headed, and here is contact information for Amy and Drew, who couldn't wait to get on the road. They wanted me to say goodbye for them and asked that you provide them your contact information so they can let you know when the baby arrives." Vic handed them each a card.

"Thank you, Dr. Vic—for the card and for your great company," Michael lifted his hand toward Dr. Vic.

"My pleasure." Dr. Vic shook Michael's hand.

"And to you, Joan—thank you for everything. It was so nice to meet you, as well," Michael continued.

"Maybe we will run into each other again in the future, but if not, it was darn nice to run into you this weekend. Take good care," Joan said as she waved her hand.

Maddie and Michael picked up their luggage and took the stroll down Belgravia and onto St. James.

"Wonder what will come of that couple," Vic remarked.

"I think something good will come of them— something real good," Joan said with a grin.

"Did I miss everyone?" Lillie asked as she came out onto the porch.

"Nope—you haven't missed Joan or me," Vic replied as he reached down to give Lillie a big hug. "Thanks for absolutely everything, Lillie. You have outdone yourself, as usual."

"I agree, Lillie! I had a wonderful time, and again, and I am grateful," and Joan offered a sincere hug, as well.

"The pleasure is always mine, and I hope you will both return. In the meantime, please travel safely."

"Bye, Lillie," Joan said as she reached for her luggage. "May I walk you to your car, Vic?"

"Absolutely," and he turned and threw a little kiss in Lillie's direction.

Lillie watched Joan and Dr. Vic walk down Belgravia. After looking around the porch and seeing that it was in good order, she walked back into the house. She stopped in the foyer to assess what needed to be done. She was already tired, having been up late cleaning after dinner then getting up early for breakfast. It was only a little past 1 o'clock on a Sunday afternoon, and she was exhausted. She had five rooms to clean and four bathrooms, but her first guest was not expected until Thursday, so she decided nothing needed to be done right away—nothing except checking on Room 3-B. She looked up the stairs, breathed in deeply and then pushed her breath out, emptying her lungs for the next breath that would get her to the second floor. She wiped the palms of her hands onto her apron and began the climb…the climb she dreaded.

Chapter 21

Lillie stood on the third-floor landing. She reached deep into her pocket, withdrew her master key and walked to 3-B. The wood floor popped with every step. She stopped, inserted the key, turned the door handle and carefully pushed the door open. She entered the sparsely furnished room. Old chairs adorned an equally old table that supported a small lamp on one side of the room, directly across from an old chest of drawers on the opposite side. The drapes of the only window were pulled, as always, and there was no bed. Lillie walked to the closet, and using the same master key, she unlocked the bolt, stepped inside and closed the door behind her. The floor creaked. Using the same master key, she re-locked the door that could be locked and unlocked on both sides only by Lillie's master key.

A narrow door inside the closet opened to a stairway that led up to the attic. Lillie walked through the door frame and began the last leg of her climb. With each step the floor creaked, interrupting the silence that now filled the inn. Lillie's view from the bottom of the stairs was of a small window at the top of the landing that offered very little light. Her incline was slow and methodical, and she didn't take the next step until the previous stair creaked. She reached the top and peered out the window. All she could see was all that she could ever see: the rooftops of other homes. She stood up straight and turned around.

It was hazy in that old attic, but at the other end was another small window offering equally little light. She could now see his silhouette, lying there in the bed and almost motionless, if not for his shallow breathing. *Was he awake or asleep?* she wondered...*or maybe dead?* which was a thought that brought a slight grin to her face.

As she approached him, she wondered what he might be thinking. She wondered if he was scared, which made her walk even slower, giving him the opportunity to suffer with anxiety as he anticipated her arrival. He would not be expecting anyone else; no one knew he was there, except the Census Bureau. No one had ever visited him, and as long as she had her way, no one ever would, although she often pondered how long she would be able to keep her secret.

She stood by his bedside, and using the limited light made available by the two small windows, she moved in closer to see if his eyes were open, and they were. "Hello, Daddy. I see you are awake."

He peered at her through tiny slits in his eyelids. By now his vision had significantly declined, but Lillie knew his memory was clear. He knew where he was, who Lillie was, and what he had done to deserve what could be described as an extremely diminished quality of life. Lillie judged that any life at all was more than he deserved.

"I would apologize if I was sorry, Daddy, but I am not sorry that you are stuck here in this attic with no friends, failing health, and a pissed-off, resentful daughter to take care of you." Her little grin reappeared. "It's Sunday, Daddy—the day I come up here and make sure you remember why you are here. To remind you of how you abused Mother and me for so many years. To shame you for the horrible way you treated us both. You don't deserve any better, Daddy."

She walked around to the other side of his bed, and his fixed eyes followed her. "Did you smell the meals this weekend, Daddy—the apple pie and homemade muffins? How about that steak on Saturday night? Oh yes, Daddy, you missed some great meals. And I had company! Remember how you never let Mother have company? She never had any friends because of you, and I'm happy that she is no longer suffering under your arrogant, self-righteous attitude. Who's sorry now, Daddy? I bet you are sorry. I hope you regret the life you led and the one you imposed upon Mother and me. I will never let you hurt me again." She paused for a moment.

"OK, Daddy, now for a health check. I see you ate your crackers and broth. I know it wasn't apple pie, but at least it was something. Do you need anything? No? Okay. Here's some fresh water." She placed it on the night table then walked around the room. "And don't pee the bed, Daddy. When that starts, things are just going to get worse." She hesitated again. "Well, I have new guests arriving soon, and I have important work to do, so bye for now." Lillie walked to the stairs, and as she began her descent, she began humming to the tune of *Hush Hush Sweet Charlotte*, and when she reached the bottom, she grinned as she removed the key from her pocket, unlocked the door that squeaked as it opened and again when it closed. There was an intentional moment of silence, then all Daddy could hear was the door being locked from the other side.

He closed his eyes and wished he would die. He knew he deserved what he was getting, but he was an old, tired, angry man with no reason to live. He never even tried to make amends when he could, and he didn't realize the value of making them now. He would live what was left of his life, lonely and miserable.

Chapter 22

Lillie continued to hum as she descended to the first floor, where she began to make her rounds, checking the house and assessing what needed to be done in preparation for her anticipated guests. She was expecting three couples by noon on Friday. Rhonda was due in the morning to help her clean and do laundry. Lillie was feeling exhausted from the hectic weekend and felt she deserved another bath.

She filled the tub with warm water and lavender bubble bath. It was a quiet afternoon meant for relaxing with the midday sun peeking through the window. She immersed herself into the water, rested her head on her bath pillow, closed her eyes, breathed a heavy sigh and attempted to de-stress.

It had been a weekend with many unanticipated chaotic moments, and Lillie longed for a normal stay, which would mean hosting guests who bring no drama and want to be left alone to their own schedules. Then she felt guilty for the thought, as she really did enjoy the group of recent guests.

Lillie appreciated the diversity of these visitors and how they all came together as strangers and ended the weekend as friends…or better. She hoped Amy and Drew's future would be as wonderful as she was imagining. She then felt excitement for Maddie and Michael, as she recalled her own experience meeting Ben for the first time, falling in love, getting married and planning a future. Now only memories, she began to wonder again how differently she had hoped things would have turned out for them.

Neither Lillie nor Ben had any concept of how time would be measured in the absence of one another. Days seemed like weeks, weeks seemed like months, and a month seemed like a year. Their youthful naiveté kept them from considering a reality they would soon discover did not lend itself to their happiness.

A Kentucky man is primed for heroism, and what better way to earn this recognition than in the armed services? Women are proud to walk beside their soldier in uniform, mothers are proud of their sons, and children are proud of their parents.

Lillie and Ben were so young when they said goodbye that hot August day so many years ago, and they had no idea it would be their last embrace. Ben received his orders, and he wore his uniform with great pride as he, Lillie and his parents stood at the bus stop waiting for Ben to be shuttled away. Ben was stoic. Training camp prepared him well, and he wore the face of a soldier off to duty with a mindset that he was strong, tough and capable. He was not going to let his country down, and he was not going to break down in front of his wife and parents.

Ben knew if he expressed concern, his new wife and mother would as well, and his father would be disappointed, so there were no tears trickling down Ben's face when he said his farewells, and fighting those tears became even harder as the bus took off down the road and his vision of Lillie became smaller and smaller until he could not see her at all.

When Lillie returned to her apartment, she lay on her bed and cried for a half hour, then she dried her tears and sat down to write her soldier husband a three-page letter. It felt to her like he had been gone for weeks already, but he had only been gone for a couple of hours by the time she signed the letter and addressed the envelope, which she set out for the mail carrier to pick up the next morning.

Ben said in his letters the first six weeks that time was going fast, but Lillie disagreed, and said it couldn't go fast enough. Lillie had missed her period in those six weeks and scheduled an appointment with her doctor. She was ridiculously excited about the possibility of having a baby—Ben's baby. She was thrilled, and she could hardly wait for confirmation so she could tell her husband, but in the meantime, she became so ill with morning sickness, she was certain of pregnancy without the doctor's test results. She wanted to share the news with her mother, but she didn't want to tell anyone until she told her husband, so she was all alone in her morning sickness, eating crackers and ice cream while also losing weight.

Two weeks before her scheduled appointment, Lillie got up in the morning and went to the kitchen to eliminate her nausea. She reached for some crackers when she doubled over in pain and finally ended up on the floor. When Lillie didn't answer her phone calls, her mother went to her apartment, and when she didn't answer the door, her mother summoned the building manager to allow her access, where she found Lillie passed out on the kitchen floor. The manager dialed 911, and an ambulance arrived and took Lillie to the hospital where she was diagnosed with an ectopic pregnancy that had perforated. Having already lost a good deal of blood, Lillie's life was in danger, and she was taken into surgery where her pregnancy was terminated, and her fallopian tubes were removed. Lillie woke up to the horrible news that her pregnancy was not viable and had been aborted in order to save her life. And then she was told the chances of her ever becoming pregnant were almost zero.

Lillie's mother was able to console her during this time, but she missed her husband. She was groggy yet stable immediately after surgery; however, she wasn't completely out of danger for a couple of days, and even after she returned home from the hospital, she was restricted from physical activity until she fully recovered and gained her strength. In the meantime, she was able to reach Ben and let him know that the good news she had hoped to share with him had turned into bad news.

Ben was as consoling as he could be from many miles away. He felt horrible for Lillie, and was distraught for them as a couple. He had wanted children desperately, as many as they could have, and he was so shocked by the sudden news that he didn't know how to respond.

He continued to write Lillie, and she wrote to him, but the tone of his letters changed over the weeks. Lillie had changed too. She was depressed with no husband to talk to, to hold her. It just wasn't natural. Lillie finally wrote Ben a letter and begged him to come home or to find a way for her to visit him, but it could never be worked out. Ben's letters started to arrive a couple times a week, then weekly, then barely a couple every month. Ben was more affected by their loss than either of them could have expected.

It was hard enough for Lillie to accept that she could never have children, but it became impossible for

Ben. He could have children, and he wanted a wife who could have them, too. It was more than their brief marriage could endure, and their divorce soon followed.

As she sat in the tub surrounded by bubbles, tiny tears streamed down her face as she recalled her brief experience as a wife and mother. It was too much for one person over a short period of time. With an abusive father, a selfish ex-husband, and a barren body, Lillie's interest in men took a downturn. She wasn't willing to become seriously involved with another man for fear that she would eventually be rejected due to her inability to bear children.

Lillie had been soaking for a half-hour. She was tired, but she had work to do, so she sat up, unplugged the tub and finished her rest, which she had determined was not that restful since it brought up so many sad memories. Lillie dried herself off, put on clean clothes and a comfy pair of slippers, and shuffled her way into the kitchen where she emptied the dishwasher and made herself a midday snack. She poured a glass of wine before she started a basket of laundry with sheets and towels in preparation for the next day's work.

The annual St. James Art Fair would officially open the upcoming weekend, the first weekend in October, and there was already scurrying in the neighborhood as vendors set up tents and prepared for the festive event. The fair is always a fabulous occasion, attracting people from all over the United States displaying their works of art. The weather is almost always perfect, and it is a day anxiously anticipated by many.

Belgravia Court would become busy with shoppers, some sipping coffee or Champagne. Most of the vendors have known the neighbors for years, though some would be new. Lillie looked forward to seeing old friends and making new ones, and she realized that if she wanted to enjoy the fair again this year, she had better get busy.

Lillie never felt sorry for herself. She was a strong and independent woman; life experiences had forced her to become strong. They also forced her to believe she needed to protect herself from further harm. Sometimes her strength left others with the perception she was reserved, antisocial, and stubborn. Lillie was unaware she had developed those appearances. In truth, she was the opposite—friendly and thoughtful, although she had developed a need to control her personal environment.

Lillie was not motivated to do laundry or any other housework, and the warm bath and glass of wine slowed her down that much more. Not typically one to procrastinate, she decided to surprise herself and put her housework off until tomorrow. She poured another glass of wine and headed for the front porch to watch the scurry of activity.

She rocked peacefully back and forth in a rocking chair with a second glass of wine in one hand while petting a cat with the other. A few neighbors passed by and waved. Vendors started to arrive, making trips to and from their cars and trucks, and Lillie was content.

Chapter 23

Sam Rossi was back again this year, with his booth immediately in front of *The Lillie Inn,* and Lillie waved when she saw him approaching. From a distance he waved back and yelled hello to her, and when he got closer, he greeted her with a big hug.

"So good to see you, Sam! Welcome back!"

"Same here, Lillie. It is good to be back."

"What's new with you? Where have you been? How is Nancy? Did she come with you?" Lillie peeked around his shoulder to see if she was on her way.

"No, Nancy did not come with me. I came straight from Illinois, and Nancy went home to get caught up on some things before the holidays. We have been very busy, and she is exhausted."

"Oh, shoot, I was looking forward to seeing her. Well, please give her my regards and let her know she was missed."

"I sure will, Lillie. So, what's new with you? Do you have guests with you today?"

"No, my weekend guests left earlier today, and I have new guests arriving on Thursday. I have a lot to do, but I needed some rest, too, so I am gifting myself with some relaxation this afternoon. Would you like to join me for a glass of wine?"

"Oh…no, thank you. The afternoon is getting away from me already. I asked about guests because I swear I saw a man peering out the window upstairs. Must have been an illusion—the direction of the sun creating shadows, and all."

"Yes…I'm sure…yes, uh…er, no, there are no guests currently. Well, Sam, if you need anything at all, please let me know. I'll see you later."

"Thank you, Lillie. I may take you up on that offer."

Lillie was fuming. *Obviously, Daddy is trying to get some attention*, she alleged. *He brings out the worst in me.* She returned to the rocking chair so as not to appear that she was reacting to Sam's remark, but she knew she needed to get upstairs soon. She finished her wine, placed the kitten on the floor of the porch, returned inside, and closed the door behind her.

She was in no frame of mind to be dealing with her dad. *Hasn't he done enough damage?* she thought. Lillie always made sure she was in possession of her master key, which she took with her as she marched up the stairs to the second floor, then the third. She was getting light-headed; her blood pressure was spiking, and she knew she needed to calm down and maintain control. She took a deep breath and regained her balance, shoved the master into the door handle of 3-B and walked in.

She closed the door behind her and leaned against it while she took another deep breath. "Breathe," she said out loud to herself. "Breathe." She unlocked the closet, walked in and locked it behind her. She grabbed a flashlight from a closet shelf and began her final ascent up the stairs. When she reached the top and turned around, she did not see his silhouette in the bed, as usual. She gazed around the small attic, expecting to find he had fallen. There was not much light at any time of day, and the late afternoon sun was preparing its descent in the west; soon it would be dark. Lillie pushed the flashlight button into the 'on' position to light her path as she slowly and carefully placed one foot in front of the other…making her way around the stair rail toward her father's bed.

She swayed the flashlight beam back and forth throughout the room while calling "Daddy? Daddy?" in an eerie, singsong tone. "I know you are here, and you know I will find you. Don't make me want to hurt you like you used to hurt me."

This was not the first time this had happened; that he tried to get some attention, but on the few occasions this had occurred, Lillie became angrier and angrier…mostly with her abusive father but also angry with herself for taking on this mission of making sure her father's final days were miserable.

The few people who ever knew her father believed he was near death in an assisted living facility, and they never cared enough about him to ask how he was doing, which was a testimony to the way he lived. Most folks could not have cared less, and Lillie only cared that she might have the opportunity to create some misery for her father in retribution for the years of pain he imposed upon her mother and herself. She was beginning to wonder who was more miserable, her father or her.

Deep down Lillie knew it was wrong, but she always managed to justify her actions every time she remembered the years of abuse. Despite her father's lack of love and nurturing, she became a compassionate person with good intentions, except when it came to him. She could not forgive him for the intentional harm he caused, and she felt vindicated by the current circumstances. Lillie figured that soon enough, her father would be gone forever, and when that time came, so too would her pain be gone.

As her search continued, she walked slowly, and listened.

"There you are, Daddy, you little devil. What do you think you are doing, you foolish, foolish man? Now I have to yank you up off the floor and get you back into the bed. It's a good thing you have become so scrawny, to make it easier for me. One of these days, you won't be a bother to me at all. You will be gone and forgotten, and no one will care whatever happened you."

She looked into his sinister eyes as she spoke to him. She turned the flashlight off and placed it in her pocket. Wrapping her arms under her father's armpits, she pulled him up and onto the bed. She knew he probably didn't need the help; after all, he managed to get himself to the window on his own, and he was able to use the facilities on his own, albeit barely. She knew he was not going to cooperate with her, so she just took control. She tucked him in, gave him fresh water and crackers and pulled the blinds on both windows. She reached into her pocket and pulled out the flashlight.

"I'm finished here, Daddy. Good night." Lillie walked down the staircase. Her father listened until he heard her unlock the closet door and exit, and relock the door behind her. He closed his eyes and prayed he would fall asleep and never wake up.

Lillie leaned against the door and breathed a heavy sigh. She made her way to the main level and to her room, where she then tucked herself into bed. She lay her head on the pillow and tried to relax. Thoughts were actively buzzing through her head, thoughts about her father and what might happen if anyone found out he was there…and being abused.

She recalled the day the assisted living facility phoned and told her that her father required a more secure environment as he had become disruptive and difficult to handle. They explained that although he was frail, he still managed to get around a bit, and now required 24-hour observation. As the only living relative, Lillie was Power of Attorney, and decisions needed to be made. She wasn't happy about paying a facility thousands of dollars for adult daycare, so she hastily decided to bring him to the inn and care for him herself.

Lillie settled her father in 2-B, but not a week had passed before she experienced the disruptive and difficult behavior of her father. She soon regretted her decision, but with so few options, she moved him to the attic where his bad behavior would not be as noticeable.

Lillie was tired of detestable men. She thought of Ben as the weak little man he had become when he learned she was barren. Lillie wondered if she would ever develop a genuine sense of appreciation for men again, which led her to thinking of Dr. Vic, who seemed to shower her with attention, but who himself seemed somewhat needy, and the last thing she wanted was another needy man. She reflected on her mother, whom she loved deeply, and a wave of sadness came over her— a feeling like her mother was present and trying to communicate.

Lillie knew she needed to get some sleep. Rhonda was expected around half-past nine in the morning and she hoped the two of them would be very productive getting the inn ready for new guests. She fell asleep listening to the bustling of a few fair vendors still preparing for the upcoming events.

Chapter 24

Lillie woke up before the alarm sounded, feeling well rested and ready to begin the day, which she did by checking in on her dad, who was fine. She started some laundry and housecleaning. Rhonda arrived right on schedule and assured their successful efforts by the end of the day.

Lillie appreciated a clean, organized and comfortable home, and she was grateful to Rhonda for sharing her vision. The two of them worked very efficiently together, and chores were complete by mid-afternoon. Lillie paid Rhonda well for her services, for which Rhonda was appreciative, though she knew she earned every penny. Lillie walked to the porch with Ronda and offered an envelope and a hug before she left for the day.

"Thanks for everything, Rhonda. You are a Godsend. See you next week!"

"My pleasure, Lillie. See you soon."

Lillie stood on the porch for a minute and admired the colorful leaves and autumn sun that blended into a picturesque creation of nature at its finest. Sam noticed her and waved, and she waved back before taking a deep, cleansing breath and returning inside. As she did, Sam directed his attention to the attic window and noticed the shades had been drawn.

The satisfaction of her clean home, coupled with the hustle and bustle of art fair preparations, stirred some excitement in Lillie, and she decided to take a walk through her gardens—her sanctuary. As she strolled through the tall grasses and wildflowers, Lillie pondered her life. She thought of the guests for whom she had provided comfortable accommodations over the years, and how much she enjoyed it. It truly was her pleasure.

She thought of her mother with deep fondness, her ex-husband Ben with a mix of sadness and disappointment, her lonely childhood without siblings, and that her life could not have been what it was and is without her father…such as it is.

Lillie had made the best of her life circumstances. She occasionally wondered what she may have sacrificed as the result of a lifetime spent protecting her wounds. She was eternally grateful to her mother and liked to think she had acquired some of her mother's good qualities like cooking and caring for others. Lillie cherished the brief experience of being in love with Ben, and she wondered if she had given up too easily on finding love again.

No one knew about her father living in the attic, if one could even call it 'living,' and Lillie intended to keep it that way; but she was tired of him and the burden he had always been. She wondered how she could even consider a romantic relationship along with the responsibility of her father. She knew it was wrong to secretly hide him in her attic like he was a frog she had found and wanted to keep. She recalled Joan Jennings and her wise words. Joan was such a thoughtful and kind person who held Lillie in high regard; if she knew about her father in the attic, surely she would think of her differently.

Joan was understanding and compassionate regarding Lillie's childhood, and she wanted to hate her father as much as Lillie did, but Joan knew hating him would only make her own life miserable, not his. Lillie also considered the possibility that she was hurting herself by holding her father hostage—that doing so was really holding herself hostage. She questioned if she would ever know true freedom until she allowed it to her father, a thought that lingered as she completed her stroll.

Frustrated by her preoccupation with vengeance, Lillie forced herself to stop her pity-party and concentrate on the arrival of her guests. She went to her room and sat at her desk to go over her guest list, menu and accommodations. She was pleased to remember that Bill and Kurt would be visiting this weekend and she smiled in anticipation. Bill and Kurt were life partners who eagerly anticipated the fair, which they attended every year. Lillie was pretty sure they were responsible for introducing the tradition of enjoying Champagne at the event.

Lillie was delighted when Bill and Kurt arrived early Thursday afternoon. Bill was pulling two pieces of luggage, and Kurt was carrying a cold bottle of Freixenet Brut in one hand and three fluted champagne glasses in the other when they walked up to the porch.

"Let the festivities begin!" insisted Kurt.

"Come in—come in! It is so good to see you two!" Lillie exclaimed, and the three retreated to the inn. Bill left the luggage in the foyer and followed Lillie and Kurt into the kitchen where Kurt was already uncorking the bottle of bubbly, and the three of them held on to the stem of their glasses while Kurt filled them up. In his normal and most appropriate fashion, Kurt raised his glass with a toast to the hostess and a blessing for a fabulous long and fun-filled weekend. The tiny clinks made by the trio of plastic glasses could barely be heard, but the sentiment was the same as if the wine had been poured into the most expensive crystal, and they all enjoyed their first sip knowing it was the beginning of a very good time for all. Following their first glass of wine, Lillie gave Bill and Kurt the keys to Room 2-A.

"Oh, yay! I love this room!" Kurt opined. He retrieved the luggage and headed up the stairs to the second floor, with Bill following him, bubbly in hand.

"Hey, Lillie, we'll meet you on the porch in ten," Bill hollered, and ten minutes later the three were sitting in rocking chairs on the porch, pouring their second glass of bubbly. Bill and Kurt insisted that Lillie bring them up to date on her life, which didn't take Lillie long, since she had little to report. Bill and Kurt then updated Lillie on their activities over the past year, which included a trip to Paris, the birth of a new niece (Kurt's sister's daughter), and the wedding of some friends in Chicago.

Bill and Kurt had been openly gay for years, and they had been a monogamous couple for the past fifteen years. They knew how to enjoy life, and they took their joy with them wherever they went. They were happy, and others were happy when they were around, which made them best-ever guests. Lillie knew that when Bill and Kurt were visiting, everyone was going to have a great time.

"Well, Lillie, we have dinner reservations at *610 Magnolia* for this evening and would love to have you join us if you are available," Bill offered, and Lillie accepted with anxious anticipation, as she had not yet dined there but knew of its excellent reputation.

"Great! Kurt and I will meet you here on the porch at seven o'clock this evening and in the meantime we're going to walk around the fair for a sneak pre-peek."

Lillie went back inside to recover a bit from her mid-afternoon bubbly, something in which she did not often indulge during a weekday. She went to her room and rested in the chair by the window with the great view of her beautiful gardens, which she had turned into a scene from *Better Homes & Gardens* magazine with party lights, cocktail and bistro tables and chairs, and a sitting area surrounding a wood-burning fire pit. It was a party weekend, and everyone would most likely be spontaneous with their plans.

As always, Lillie had a fridge full of lunch meat, salads, water and soda, and she would offer a continental breakfast on Saturday and Sunday. She had done an outstanding job of making her inn warm, welcoming, and accommodating. Confident she had provided well for her guests, she felt comfortable in allowing herself to have some fun, and her recent self-reflection made it clear to her that this was something she was definitely lacking in her life.

As she rested, Bill and Kurt perused the exhibits and identified as best they could those they wanted to visit again when the fair officially opened. They were pleased to recognize some familiar faces from previous shows, as well as some first-time vendors. It was a perfect day for a walk with a glass of Champagne, and they discussed how fortunate they were to have the time to attend the fair and visit good friends.

They returned to the inn, unpacked their luggage and got settled in their room. Before they knew it, it was six-thirty and they needed to prepare for dinner. Bill and Kurt were very handsome and made a striking couple. Bill was six feet tall with dark hair and blue eyes, and his charismatic appearance often caught the eye of many a passerby. He always dressed to the nines and appeared as if he had just walked out of *GQ* magazine. Bill had blond hair, blue eyes, and at six foot one, he was barely taller than Kurt. He, too, was always superbly dressed, and tonight would be no exception. The two men were patiently waiting on the porch when Lillie arrived at seven o'clock. Knowing she would be dining with two of the best-dressed men in Louisville, she chose a festive frock with metallic detail, which she wore with embellished ballet slippers. On her tiny figure with her hair pulled back, she was sure to turn some heads, though that was not her intention; her only hope was to not embarrass her friends, a goal she far exceeded.

Kurt and Bill could not have been more complimentary to Lillie, and they each offered an arm to escort her to dinner, which was in walking distance. Sam was still setting up his exhibit as they walked by and acknowledged him. He almost didn't recognize Lillie, and he could hardly take his eyes off of her as they walked down the street.

Dinner was sensational. 610 Magnolia fulfilled expectations with a diverse and interesting menu and an excellent wine selection. Completely satisfied, the three returned to the inn by ten o'clock. Exhausted from a fabulous day, they soon retired for the evening.

Chapter 25

Friday promised to be a busy day with new guests arriving in the morning and the official opening of the art fair. This was a favorite weekend for most of Old Louisville, where new friendships are made and old ones renewed. It was with anxious anticipation that Lillie welcomed her guests on this particular weekend, one of her personal favorites.

Lillie was up by 6 o'clock Friday morning. She showered and prepared for her day, which, like most days, began in the kitchen. It wasn't long before the scent of cinnamon had created a swirl of enticing aroma around the kitchen, into the dining room and living room, up the stairs and under the doors of the guest rooms, and very likely all the way to the attic where her father could only salivate. The aroma served as an alarm clock for Bill and Kurt, who followed it back down the stairs where they found coffee, juice, fruit, and cereal along with the cinnamon rolls smothered in icing.

"Lillie, this is perfect!" Bill opined, and he and Kurt filled their plates and coffee cups and took them to the porch to enjoy. The vendors were eagerly placing the finishing touches on their exhibits as they prepared for their first customers. The air was cool and crisp, though the sun had already started to warm up the day. The news promised perfect weather for the fair and no one was more grateful than the vendors.

Lillie soon came out with a plate of food and hot coffee, which she delivered in usual Kentucky-friendly fashion to Sam, who was much obliged. The two chatted for a few minutes before Lillie retreated to the inn, and as she walked away Sam was reminded of her stunning beauty he had witnessed the previous night.

By noon all guests had arrived. Clint and Fancy Brown from Lexington in 2-B, Mel and Abby Noonan, friends of the Browns and also from Lexington, in 2-C, Cecily Jane, an artist and vendor from Cotati, California, whose booth was on St. James Court, stayed in room 3-A, and Kyle and Karen Williams, from Indianapolis, friends of Lillie's neighbors on Hill Street, occupied 3-C.

The fair officially opened at 10 o'clock. Lillie knew her guests would be coming and going throughout the weekend, busy with shopping, visiting, partying, and creating new memories. The quality of merchandise available from the vendors was outstanding, and Sam's booth in particular created quite a crowd as folks gathered to examine his sculptures. He was a talented artist whose works of art captured profound emotion—so much so that it was common to be moved to tears in the presence of his work. Lillie enjoyed sitting on the porch greeting guests, neighbors, and shoppers…sipping on her coffee, listening to the music from the trio of instrumentalists performing in the center of the walking court, hearing bits and pieces of conversations about the exhibits, and people-watching in general. This was a weekend she always enjoyed, especially when the weather was so accommodating.

The traffic had been heavy all day, and she noticed that Sam didn't get much of a break, but as the day came to a close and traffic diminished, Lillie went down to chat with him.

"How is it going? Looks to me like you have received a good deal of attention today!" she commented.

"It has been a good day, Lillie. Thanks for asking. I am exhausted, though."

"I bet you are! May I offer you some respite? I have some food and drink and a relaxing environment…not to mention, good company."

"That sounds very nice, but I need to close up my booth and get ready for tomorrow—and I really should get back to my hotel and rest for what I expect will be an even busier day tomorrow."

"I understand, but the offer remains open, and I hope you change your mind. You know where you can find me." As she headed back to the porch, Lillie stopped and talked to some neighbors before going inside where it was quiet.

Lillie was well prepared for her guests this weekend, and since they were essentially on their own, she was on her own, as well. She checked in on her father earlier, and she would check on him again before going to bed, so she poured herself a glass of wine and headed out to the gardens and sit by the fire.

The Browns and the Noonans were already at the garden showing each other the items they purchased at the fair and discussing places to eat dinner. Lillie arrived and having overheard them, suggested 610 Magnolia if they were interested in a fine dining experience with an interesting urban menu. She then offered them a list of several other options within a short drive. They chatted for a bit and the guests excused themselves to prepare for dinner.

Lillie enjoyed meeting new people and reacquainting with past friendships, but she quickly realized that at some point everyone left. Her mother left, her unborn baby left, Ben left, and weekend after weekend her guests left. They leave her with great memories and experiences, but the pattern was clear: everyone leaves. Lillie had no idea why this just occurred to her, but she began to feel oddly cold and nauseated. She looked beautiful sitting there by the crackling fire under the moonlit sky with her long brown hair blowing gently in the evening breeze. She could hear voices all blending together…shoppers purchasing their final items for the day and vendors preparing to close their booths, tallying their inventory and happy to bring this long day to an end.

Lillie got up and walked out to the porch so she could put some faces to the voices. She gazed around at the thinning crowd. The air was crisp and smelled wet like dew settling on the leaves. The neighborhood cats were finding their way through the neighborhood to determine with whom they would spend the night, and Lillie was always happy when she was chosen; in preparation she had food and water available at the corner of the porch. As these thoughts were dancing in her head, she realized that even the cats leave.

She was pondering her thoughts when she heard someone calling her name.

"Lillie?"

"Yes. Oh, Sam—hello! I'm so sorry. I was lost in my thoughts."

"I'm sorry to interrupt, but I reconsidered your earlier invitation," he said with a smile. "If the offer is still open, I would love to join you this evening."

"That's—well—that's great! Come in. Please."

"I'll be right up. I just need to close up my tent."

"I'll pour you some wine. Red or white?"

"I'll have what you're drinking, Lillie. Thank you!"

Sam closed his tent and headed up to the porch where cats were eating and purring and where a gentle breeze was causing the rocking chairs to sway. Sam appreciated how comfortable and welcoming the porch appeared, and as he looked up, Lillie was standing at the door with a glass of pinot noir in each hand.

"Let me get the door for you, Lillie."

"Thank you, Sam. Do you prefer the porch, the living room, or fireside in the back gardens?"

"Wow! Great options, and fireside sounds very inviting."

Sam entered the foyer where he gratefully accepted his glass of wine and followed Lillie through the dining room and into the kitchen. In one fell swoop, Lillie gracefully plucked up the half-full bottle of wine from the counter before leading Sam out the back door into the gardens.

"This is lovely, Lillie. I don't think I have ever been back here."

"Thank you, Sam. Please, make yourself comfortable," as she patted her hand on the seat next to her. "I'm sure you are tired."

Sam settled in. He leaned toward Lillie and raised his glass, and took a sip.

"Mmmmmm. So good, Lillie. Thank you again."

"My pleasure."

Lillie and Sam sat and talked for almost an hour, though it flew by. When Lillie looked at her watch and realized it was almost eight o'clock, she couldn't believe it.

"Oh my, Sam. It is definitely dinnertime, and I have a ton of food. Please eat with me." Sam accepted and followed her into the kitchen where he took a seat while Lillie pulled prepared food out of the fridge along with bread, cheese, chips and fruit. Lillie created quite a spread, and the two of them spent the next hour in the kitchen nibbling on homemade chicken salad, sweet coleslaw, and chips. They were deeply engaged in conversation and getting to know one another better. Sam didn't notice that Lillie had opened a second bottle of wine.

Sam explained that he and Nancy were no longer together. Lillie had assumed they were married, but Sam explained otherwise. He revealed they had been together for years but decided recently to part ways, and he didn't see the point in going into all of that earlier when Lillie asked about Nancy. He added that their relationship just ran its course.

Lillie also learned that Sam was forty-three, had never been married and had no children. Of Italian descent, he was incredibly handsome. He was six feet tall with a head full of black curls and just long enough to identify him as an artist. His blue eyes were like the ocean, and his lips were simply kissable. Lillie could not imagine that this man would be alone for long.

By his own admission, Sam's life's work and focus was his sculpting, which was exquisite, an opinion shared by many (not just Lillie). The St. James Art Fair Association collectively believed it was an honor that Sam chose to exhibit his work at the fair, as he had become highly regarded by his peers in the industry, though Sam attributed much of his success to that which he found at St. James Art Fair, as well as others.

Lillie discovered that Sam lived most of his life in Santa Barbara, California, with his parents, two sisters and a brother, and he shared some heartwarming stories of growing up in his family with much love and support. He missed them immensely and was considering a visit to California after the first of the year. Lillie was charmed with Sam's gifted sense of humor, and at this point she was unable to find one thing about him she didn't like.

Time continued to fly by, and by now they were finished eating, however they continued to sip on the wine. Sam helped Lillie tidy up the kitchen, just another quality she appreciated in him, and she began wondering to herself if he was too good to be true. She stared into his beautiful eyes, imagining what she didn't know about him, like how it would feel to run her fingers through his thick, curly hair or to glide them gently across the dark stubble on his handsome face. As he sipped his wine, she watched his strong hands and considered how gentle they must also be to sculpt works of art that arouse such deep passion. What she didn't notice was how mesmerized she had become. Her bottom lip slightly parted from her top lip and she felt an impulse to reach out and touch Sam's hands with which she had become so enamored.

"Lillie? Lillie? Are you alright?"

"Um—ye—yes, I'm fine. Why? Oh, I'm so sorry Sam. Must be the wine. What did you ask?" She replied as she felt the blood rush to her now rosy cheeks.

"I asked if you could point me in the direction of the bathroom."

"Of course," she replied.

The closest bathroom was in Lillie's en suite, and she showed him the way and returned to the kitchen. It didn't occur to her until later how suggestive it may have been to introduce Sam to her en suite, her personal space.

Lillie was a bit embarrassed, realizing how taken she was with Sam. There had been very few men since her marriage to Ben, and the few were casual and almost forgotten. She had known Sam for years, but she had known him as a half of Sam and Nancy, so she never thought of him as anything but a friend. Today she found herself wanting more.

Lillie had become accustomed to avoiding relationships. She wasn't consciously aware that she was capable of the type of feelings she was experiencing with Sam. Between her strong urges and the consumption of wine, she found herself losing control of her otherwise clear thinking and reasonable decision-making skills.

Lillie was sitting on a barstool at the kitchen island when Sam returned.

"Are you doing okay, Lillie?" Sam asked as he approached her.

"Yes—yes, I'm doing fine."

"Well, I guess we need to call it a day. Tomorrow will be here all too soon."

Lillie stood up and Sam approached her, taking her hands and thanking her for her kind hospitality.

"You are very generous, Lillie. I hope you take as good care of yourself as you do others." He lowered her hands and stepped in to give her a hug.

"Thank you, Sam; it is always my pleasure. I appreciate this chance to get to know you better. I'm quite impressed." They stepped back from each other.

"I need to go. My car is in the back alley, and it's a twenty-minute drive to the hotel. I'll see you tomorrow, Lillie. Thank you again."

Lillie smiled. "I wish you were staying here."

Sam was a little taken aback, which was apparent by the look on his face.

Lillie giggled. "I mean if you were staying at my inn, you would already be at your destination by now."

Sam laughed, too, and he now felt a bit embarrassed for having misunderstood Lillie's remark.

"Truth is, Sam, I do wish you were staying here—for the exact reason you were thinking."

Sam smiled again, walked toward Lillie and placed his arms around her. Lillie tried to remain strong as she paused to discern if his intentions were the same as hers. Sam held her for a minute, considering Lillie's invitation. He had thoroughly enjoyed his evening with her, as well, but he did not want to take advantage of her.

"Lillie, I would love to stay." Sam felt Lillie melt into his arms. He looked down at Lillie as she was looking up at him. She reached her hand up and ran her fingers through his hair.

"I've wanted to do that all evening," she whispered.

Sam leaned down and kissed Lillie, who had also been longing to experience his lips touching hers, and she was pleased…so much so, she couldn't remain quiet and her tiny moans revealed her pleasure. Her body was covered in goose bumps and she shivered. Lillie gently broke their embrace, took Sam's hand, guided him back to her en suite and closed the door.

Lillie was a beautiful woman, although she rarely focused on her physical beauty. Her heart was pure, and the beauty within was reflected in her presence. Sam was suddenly seeing her for the first time.

The lights were dimmed. Lillie walked to the window and pulled the blinds. She turned and walked toward Sam, and standing in front of him, she unbuttoned her dress until it was loose enough to fall to the floor, revealing her beautiful ivory-colored skin covered only by a pink lace bra and panties. She reached up and pulled a pin from her hair, allowing her long dark locks to fall on her tiny shoulders and down her back. She reached both hands up to stroke Sam's stubbly face.

Sam couldn't take his eyes off Lillie. He saw before him a beautiful woman with flawless skin that longed to be touched and lips he ached to kiss. He sensed her heart was pure and filled with genuinely good intentions. He had come to know her beauty inside, and now he was seeing how it manifested on the outside. He took her hands into his, brought them to his lips and kissed them gently then placed them on his chest. Lillie proceeded to unbutton his shirt before sliding it off of his broad shoulders. She touched his bare chest with her fingertips and then nuzzled her face onto it and breathed in his scent. Sam removed his trousers before tenderly placing Lillie on her bed, then he lay down next to her, gliding his hands up and down her curved, soft skin. He removed her bra and panties so skillfully Lillie hardly noticed.

Sam was in awe of her body-so petite, so perfect, and so warm. Lillie reached for Sam's face and guided his lips to hers, and the kiss was passionate. Strong, yet soft. Lillie's arms were wrapped around Sam while she, too, stroked his beautiful body around his sculpted shoulders and down his back. She tugged at the waistband of his boxers to hint they be removed; Sam was accommodating, and Lillie could not have been more pleased.

Lillie became weak all over. She wanted Sam…all of him, and she wanted him now. She yearned for him, she moaned for him, and she reached for him. Sam leaned in and kissed Lillie's face, then her neck, then her breasts. Filled with eager anticipation, Lillie could barely breathe.

Sam wanted Lillie, too. All of her. He turned her over so he could kiss every inch of her soft skin…across her shoulders, down her back and perfectly round bottom. Lillie was squirming with delight. When Sam returned her to her back, the smile on her face almost melted him. Lillie reached for Sam to come closer and begged him to take her now. He teased her for a moment, making her beg again, which she did. Then he wrapped Lillie up in his arms and thrust himself into her until they were both moaning with passionate satisfaction.

Sam rolled to his side without letting go of Lillie. She curled up in his arms, and the two were now one. Words were inadequate, so none were spoken, and they both fell into the best night's sleep either had had in months.

Chapter 26

Morning came early for Lillie. She awoke at five o'clock and gazed at Sam, still sound asleep, and she wondered if there was ever a time when he wasn't as handsome as in that moment. She stroked his shoulder then buried her face in his chest to savor his scent one more time. She realized that today was Sunday and the last day of the fair. Sam had talked about moving back to California, and Lillie didn't know if she would ever see him again, but she knew she wanted to. It was only one night, she thought, and she encouraged herself to enjoy the moment, even though it may never be repeated.

When Sam awoke, Lillie had been in and out of the shower, dressed and in the kitchen with her hair up and wearing an apron as she prepared breakfast. Cecily had already grabbed some Danish and coffee to go before heading to her booth. The Browns and the Noonans were taking their time before venturing out for their last day of the fair, and Bill and Kurt were on their way down to the dining room, hoping Lillie was serving Mimosas this morning, and once again, they were not disappointed.

"Good morning!" Bill greeted Lillie, who replied with the same.

"You were reading our minds, Lillie! I see Mimosas are available. You are the best!" They all laughed.

Mimosas were poured, and toasts had been made when Sam entered the kitchen from Lillie's room. His entrance was noticed.

"Mmmmm—Lillie! I'm impressed!" Kurt declared.

Lillie smiled and winked.

"You don't think I was going to let you guys dress her up and take her to dinner without noticing, did you?" Sam asked, and everyone laughed. Kurt handed Sam a

Mimosa and they all toasted. Nothing more needed to be said.

Sam needed to get his booth ready, but he was embarrassed to wear the same clothes as yesterday. Not to his surprise, Lillie washed them after her shower, and Sam was grateful.

After another Mimosa, Sam excused himself to tend to his booth. He promised Lillie he would touch base with her later.

Bill and Kurt were determined to get more information from Lillie about her night, but she was saved by the arrival of the Browns and Noonans for breakfast, and they too were interested in the Mimosas. After she felt her presence was no longer necessary, she excused herself and returned to her room. The guests took their Mimosas and coffee out to the gardens and enjoyed one last opportunity to sit by the fire on this crisp autumn morning.

It was another beautiful day. The sun was shining, the dewdrops on the foliage were lifting, and the fire was crackling. Music could be heard in the distance, and the smell of caramel corn was wafting through the air. As the guests gathered, they commented on the perfect place to enjoy the fair and considered themselves fortunate.

Lillie cracked her bedroom window so she could allow some of the outside into her room. There was a sense of contentment about her, and she could not take her mind off of the events of last night.

Lillie knew deep down that owning and operating a bed and breakfast would assure her of no time for a serious, romantic relationship. However, if she were to entertain the unlikely possibility, Sam would most definitely be her first choice. He had it all—he was handsome, healthy, successful, and most importantly, available. But Lillie shied away from such connections, and she rather expected that Sam would do the same since his latest love interest had been so recent. Lillie knew she needed to focus on other things.

All the guests were now on the *fair trail*, and Lillie tidied up the remains of breakfast. The inn was quiet, and Lillie decided this was a good time to check on her father. She was exhausted just thinking about it.

She took her normal path to the attic, carrying a basket of items to replenish his nutrition supply. Every step was a burden. Last night she experienced her highest high, and at this moment she was experiencing her lowest of lows.

At the time her father took ill, her mother had already passed, and Lillie was the only person who could help him. She hated him so much; she could scarcely imagine her feeding her father, much less cleaning up after him. She was angry. Her mother and best friend was gone. Her husband was gone. She was immersed in her work at the inn, and for good reason. She didn't have much of a life otherwise. Now she had to consider sharing her life with the one person she despised more than any other…the one person who had intentionally harmed her mother and her when they were unable to protect themselves.

How was she to care for him, when he never cared for her? How long was he going to live, anyway? Her thoughts were screaming inside her head. She sat down on a step leading to the attic and held her head, hoping to quiet her wild imaginings, and she started to cry.

When her contemplations quieted enough that she was able to think more clearly, she realized she had become her own worst enemy, that she was creating this situation and her own pain. She felt guilty about holding her father captive. She knew that despite all of his wrong doing, she had no right to make things worse. What would Sam think if he knew she was holding her father hostage, for heaven's sake? What would Joan think? What would Bill and Kurt think? *Anyone would understand my anger,* she thought, *but could I really justify this behavior?*

Her father had not laid a hand on her for years, and now he was likely more terrified of her than she ever was of him.

"What in the hell have I been thinking?" she screamed out loud to herself in the narrow stairwell. "My God—what am I doing?"

Lillie realized that denying her father proper care made her no better than him, but she didn't know how to rectify the situation. She recognized that while she essentially imprisoned her father, she was being held hostage, too. *How can I have so much love in my heart and be filled with so much hate at the same time?* she asked herself. Lillie knew there was no justification for her father's behavior, and as hard as she tried, she knew there was no justification for hers either. She knew that "two wrongs don't make a right" which her mother had repeated to her throughout her childhood. She was overcome with nausea as she considered how she might bring herself to be kind toward this man she had come to know as a monster.

She stopped feeling sorry for herself, dried her tears, and finished her journey to the attic. She opened the blind at the top of the stairs and let the sun shine in. She walked to her father's bedside and stood there looking at him while he stared back through his beady eyes filled with fear.

"We need to talk."

Lillie walked to the window at the opposite end of the attic and opened the blind. It was the brightest it had been in the attic since he arrived a year ago. She returned to the bedside and pulled up a chair.

"Can you hear me?" she asked, but he didn't answer.

"I know you can hear me, but I need you to acknowledge me—now!" He nodded his head.

"I know you are afraid. It has been my intention to make you as scared of me as you made Mama and me all those years. But no more. This is over. I'm tired. I'm tired of the haunting memories you remind me of; I'm tired of your continued imposition on every day of my life. It has to end now—in this moment."

He was confused. He didn't know what end meant.

Was she going to kill him now and finally put him out of his misery? Lillie could see his fear and confusion.

"I am so angry at you." Her eyes filled with tears. "You hurt Mama and me so much and for so long, and I wanted to hurt you back. But I'm exhausted. Hurting you is hurting me. I don't feel better when you feel bad—I feel bad too."

Her father's eyes also filled with tears that trickled down his cheeks. He knew there was little time left, but he didn't know what was going to happen. Lillie didn't know if his tears were from feeling sorry for himself or if he was sorry for the horrible things he had done throughout his life. Either way, she got no satisfaction from watching him weep.

Lillie stopped talking and propped her father up in bed with some pillows. He was pretty scrawny, in part due to his poor diet. Lillie had provided him minimal fodder for the past year making sure he had enough nutrition to sustain him, but she intentionally disallowed him the pleasure of a quality dining experience. "I'll bring you some lunch" she said and headed back downstairs, certain that her father was contemplating his "last supper".

Moments later, Lillie returned with a bowl of chicken soup, crackers and fresh fruit on a bed tray that she rested over his lap. "Eat up" she ordered, "while I prepare you a room downstairs." He peered at her as she left him alone in the sunlit room as if she could not be trusted.

Lillie descended the stairs feeling somewhat lighter. Admitting to herself that her vengeance-seeking plan was not in alignment with her true intention to be a good person, she had begun the real process of her own healing. Revenge didn't change the past and make her well; in fact, it made her as bad as he. She knew she would find new freedom when her father was given his. She was apprehensive about how things would go, but she believed she was doing the right thing, and in all other areas of Lillie's life, she strove to always do the right thing.

Lillie entered Room 3-B from the closet and closed the doors behind her. She stood in the room for a moment and envisioned how she would redecorate the room and offer it to guests. She returned to the kitchen, where she found notes from the Browns, the Noonans, and the Williams, who had checked out. She peeked out the front door and watched Sam interacting with customers. He was so friendly and easy to talk to, and shivers went up and down her spine as she was reminded of last night's events.

"Aww, Lillie. He is a sight for sore eyes, to be sure," Kurt opined as he walked up behind her. Lillie was startled and turned around quickly, and Kurt winked at her. Lillie walked out onto the porch with Kurt and Bill.

"Dear Lillie, we must get going. We had a blast this weekend. You are innkeeper extraordinaire, and we are grateful!" Lillie laughed and hugged her friends goodbye. She watched them get lost in the crowd as they walked toward the court. She caught Sam looking at her and she waved.

Cecily was the only guest not yet checked out and it would be five o'clock this evening before she would close her booth, and probably seven o'clock before she departs. It was mid-afternoon now, and Lillie hoped Sam would be taking a break soon so they could touch base, as he promised. She retreated to her room where she sat at her desk and began searching for resources to help her with her father. She would make an appointment with his physician tomorrow for a physical, and she made a list of nursing homes and assisted living facilities to contact for information. She couldn't wait until he was gone.

Once finished, Lillie went to the second floor and began cleaning 2-A, where she decided she would move her father in the meantime. She scrubbed the bathroom, dusted, and changed the sheets. Rhonda would be arriving tomorrow to help her with the rest of the cleaning, and Lillie considered how she would tell Rhonda about her father who had been living miserably in her attic for just over a year . . . or how she would tell anyone, for that matter . . . or *if* she would tell anyone.

She heard the screen door close and was delighted to see Sam standing in the foyer as she descended the stairs.

"Are you here to touch base?" she asked as she batted her eyes.

"Darn right, but I'd rather touch you," he replied, and he reached to embrace her.

"Do you have some time to sit and talk?" Lillie asked.

"I really don't, since there is no one to watch my booth for me. I have done very well, and the traffic is progressively slowing down, so I could close early, like around four o'clock. Then maybe we can get a bite to eat and talk."

Lillie knew that would have to work, and it gave her about two hours to relocate her father, assuming she would be able to get him down two flights of stairs by herself. Lillie offered Sam food and drink, and he returned to his booth. The crowd had thinned considerably, and Sam was able to organize for closing.

For the first time Lillie ascended the stairs to the attic without trepidation. She found no pleasure from seeing her father squirm, although she felt he deserved it. When she reached the attic, she found her father sitting in a chair next to the window watching the fair come to a close. Lillie hoped this meant he was strong enough to make his way downstairs.

"Are you ready to move?"

He nodded and slowly stood up and walked toward her.

"Good. I will help you. The attic steps are steep but they widen on the third floor." She placed one of his hands on the rail and tucked the other in her elbow.

Together they took one step at a time until they reached the third floor and exited the attic into 3-B. From there they exited onto the landing and proceeded to descend the stairs again, in the same fashion, to the second floor. Once on the second floor, Lillie guided her father to 2-A and opened the door. The room was warm, welcoming and smelled of lavender. The drapes were pulled, and the sun was making its way to the west where it would soon disappear.

Lillie walked him to a chair and helped him sit. He was winded from the long journey, but Lillie could sense he was relieved, and she was too.

"Are you hungry? I have plenty to eat. What sounds good?"

"Meat," he replied.

Lillie placed a blanket on his lap and left for the kitchen, returning with a tray of chicken salad, fruit, and water. It had been a while since he had a substantial meal, and she thought it best to take it easy. She placed his meal on a TV tray already in the room, and she sat in the chair next to him as he ate. By the time he finished, he was exhausted. Lillie removed his tray.

"You need to rest; do you want to use the bathroom?"

"Yes," he replied with a lisp, and Lillie added dentist to her list of things to do.

She dreaded the day she would have to assist him in the restroom, and she prayed all he needed right now was assistance to the commode.

"Let me know when you are finished, and I will help you back to bed." She waited a minute, and when she thought he was fine, she took the food tray back to the kitchen. When she returned to the room, she found her father sitting on the edge of the bed, and she breathed a sigh of relief.

"You're in good condition." She helped pull his legs up onto the bed, plumped up his pillows and tucked him in. "Just because you are able to get around, please don't try to manage the stairs by yourself. You should have everything you need in this room, and I will check on you periodically, but I don't think you are strong enough to manage the stairs by yourself. Okay?" He nodded.

"Would you like some music or TV?" Lillie asked.

"Music. I can't see good," he replied, and Lillie added ophthalmologist to her list. She turned on the iPod and played music from a playlist that Mama used to listen to. Daddy closed his eyes, and it wasn't long before he was lulled to sleep.

It was five o'clock before Sam finished closing his booth. He returned his inventory to his truck and was packed and ready to go. When he entered the inn, Lillie was waiting for him. They both were exhausted.

"You look tired, Lillie. Are you okay?"

"Yes…probably better than ever, really, but it has been quite a weekend, and the week ahead promises to be a long one."

"Well, I have time to listen if you want to talk."

Lillie was reluctant to tell Sam about her father, and right now she didn't need to, so she thanked him for his concern, but the only thing she wanted to talk about was the two of them.

"Lillie, this was the most memorable St. James Art Fair that I can recall, thanks to you!"

"For me, too," she replied.

"So—what does it mean? I don't know, but I like being with you and would love to visit again . . . soon."

"I'm so glad, Sam, because I feel the same."

They were sitting in the front room when Cecily walked in.

"Hi, Cecily. How are you? How did you do?" Lillie asked.

"Exhausted but good!" she replied. "I'm finally packed up and ready to go, Lillie. Thank you again for your generosity and allowing me to extend my stay."

"Always my pleasure," Lillie responded, and they hugged. "Until next year," Lillie said.

Cecily told both Lillie and Sam goodbye and left.

"It's just you and me, Lillie, and I need to go, too. I can't wait to see you again, and it will be well before this time next year!"

They stood up and embraced. Neither of them wanted to let go, but both were tired with busy schedules for the days ahead.

"One step—one step at a time," Lillie remarked.

With some hesitancy, Sam left, and Lillie watched him until he disappeared up the street. Vendors were still breaking down their displays. The only music was that made by the fountain on St. James Court. Several folks gathered at the court after the fair ended, so there was still some crowd noise.

A couple of neighborhood kittens were rubbing against her ankles, and she leaned down, picked one up and sat in a rocking chair. Lillie took a deep breath . . . exhaled and repeated out loud: "One step, one step at a time."

Chapter 27

As she sat and reflected, Lillie knew she deserved to be loved. Her romantic interlude with Sam was a moment in time she hoped would repeat itself many times in the future, and if he didn't contact her, she would definitely contact him, but not until after she handled her father.

Lillie realized the year of holding her father hostage would be perceived as sinister by most. She vacillated between what was right and wrong, but she was beginning to recognize that no good had come from her behavior. Lillie had never considered herself a vengeful person, and she was not feeling good about what she had been doing. She was emotionally wounded, but she also knew her father must have been, too. *Enough already*, she thought.

Lillie went inside to close-up the inn. After she ensured the house was locked up, she went in to check on her father, who was sound asleep. She backed out of the room and quietly closed the door.

When Lillie walked into her room she was certain she heard her bed calling her name. She was so tired and could hardly wait to get under the covers, and when she did, she immediately fell asleep.

Lillie was never afraid in her inn, her home and safe haven, where she was most comfortable. She had a good security system, and while many friends and guests, as well as some strangers, had come and gone, she always felt secure there. Tonight, she felt even safer, knowing she no longer had to be concerned about the status of her father. He was warm and cozy in a room with more than adequate provisions, and it gave Lillie some relief knowing she would soon be freed of her well-kept secret. She was looking forward to no more questions about the noises on the third floor or scheduling visits to her father in the attic at times when her absence would not be noticed.

Lillie was up before the sun on Monday morning and was a little anxious, knowing she had a demanding day ahead. Rhonda was due to arrive early, and Lillie needed to be prepared to explain her 'new guest.' She took a quick shower and dressed before venturing out of her room. Her first task was to check on her father.

Lillie looked up the first flight of stairs and much to her surprise, she saw her father standing unsteadily at the top. He was scrawny, disheveled, and disoriented. Lillie knew she was trying to do the right thing with him, but she despised him with such intensity, looking at him standing there so pathetic did not endear him to her.

"Daddy," she said, "stay right where you are. You don't have the strength to come down the steps by yourself. Please let me help you." As she began to climb the stairs, her father moved as if to attempt the descent on his own. Lillie looked up and saw her father tottering. "Daddy! No!" She hurried to reach him, and as many times as she had climbed hundreds of stairs every day since she owned the inn, no climb seemed as long as this one.

As she hurried up the stairs, with only a few steps to go, Lillie held her arms up, shouting, "No! Stop! Stop, Daddy!" But it was to no avail. He missed his mark, stumbled and fell right onto Lillie, and the two of them went tumbling down the flight of stairs, a tangled mess of legs and arms flailing as their bodies rolled over one another with thumping sounds and agonizing moans and groans until they hit the landing with thud after thud followed by total silence.

Lillie landed face down on the foyer where she lay for several minutes before she came to. Somewhat incoherent and moaning in pain as she attempted to move, she raised her head slightly and opened her eyes to find herself face to face with her father.

"Daddy?" Lillie asked in a tiny voice that was all she could muster.

There was no answer.

"Daddy?" she asked again.

Again, no answer.

"Shit." She passed out again.

Chapter 28

Rhonda rang the doorbell. She had a key, yet she always rang the bell to let Lillie know she had arrived, but never waited for Lillie to answer the door. She unlocked it and attempted to open it, but it was obstructed. Rhonda applied some more pressure. She managed to get the door open enough to yell for Lillie, and when she did, she heard some moaning. She kept pushing the door against, what turned out to be, the body of Lillie's father. As she continued to push, his face was forced closer and closer to Lillie's. Rhonda was able to poke her head inside to see them both lying on the floor.

"Oh my God, Lillie! Lillie! Are you okay? Oh my God!"

Rhonda forced her way into the foyer, leaned over Lillie and called her name repeatedly until Lillie responded. The thoughts going through Rhonda's head were aplenty: *Who was this man? What the hell happened? Was he trying to hurt her? What should I do?* Rhonda dialed 911.

Lillie's father was pronounced dead by the paramedics, and Lillie was taken to the ER by ambulance. The police stayed to investigate the scene, and Rhonda helped the best she could, not knowing what had taken place.

There were two police officers, a man and a woman, both tough as nails, and both assumed Rhonda knew more than she did. They apparently felt that since she had a key to the inn, she was more familiar with the situation than she was trying to make them believe.

"So, Rhonda, tell us what you know," Officer Matt insisted.

"Uh, I don't know anything—at least not about this situation. I know Lillie, who owns this inn, but I have no clue who the man is. I have never seen him before."

Rhonda went on to explain she worked for Lillie, the innkeeper. She told them she works only on Mondays unless there is a special occasion, and as far as she knew, there was no special occasion except for the art fair that had just ended, and she understood all of the guests would have been checked out by yesterday. She reiterated she knew nothing of this man who was found dead on the floor, but that she could show the officers around the inn.

They began their tour on the first floor, and other than the scene of the 'alleged' accident, there were no findings that were suspect. Lillie's room was neat and tidy as usual, her bed had been made and the drapes were pulled. Rhonda led the way up the stairs to the second floor, during which time she explained there were three floors with three rooms each on level two and level three.

The first room examined was 2-A. Because Rhonda was aware that all the rooms on the second floor had been reserved over the weekend, she was not surprised when Officer Matt found clear evidence that the room had been occupied.

"I expect you will find all of the rooms have been recently occupied. That is why I work here on Mondays—to help clean following the departure of guests and to prepare the rooms for incoming guests. I remove the sheets and towels, launder them, clean the rooms, and replace the linens."

"Is it common to find food in the rooms after the guests have left?" Officer Sandy asked.

"Yes," Rhonda replied. "However, Lillie usually goes through the rooms on Sundays after all the guests have checked out and removes any food or dishes." She noticed Officer Sandy made a note.

Rhonda continued to lead the tour. The officers were thorough in their investigation, looking under beds, in closets and showers, behind doors, in drawers—even behind wall hangings—but they found nothing suspicious.

When they investigated the third floor, they noticed the difference in the layout of the three rooms and one bath, all of which were examined with the same thoroughness. Officer Matt found it curious that 3-B was not fully furnished with a bed for overnight guests, and Rhonda explained that Lillie had not reserved that room for several years, though she couldn't explain why, which piqued Officer Matt's curiosity, and he nodded to Officer Sandy, who made another entry in her notepad.

Officer Matt then walked to the closet, opened the door and stuck his head inside. He reached up and pulled a chain that turned on a light. He saw some blankets folded neatly on a shelf and a couple of items hanging from the clothes rack. He also noticed a flashlight on the shelf next to the blankets, but he had observed that all of the rooms had a flashlight in the closet. What he did not detect was the well-hidden door to the attic.

Almost an hour had passed, and the tour of the inn was completed. Officers Matt and Sandy thanked Rhonda for her assistance and said they were going to check the grounds to see if they might find something that could provide a clue. When they finished fifteen minutes later, they found Rhonda on the porch talking with some of the neighbors who were conducting their own query after noticing the emergency vehicles. Rhonda explained what she could, but that right now, Lillie was the only person who could provide accurate information.

"Rhonda?" Officer Sandy asked.

"Yes, Officer?"

"Thank you for your assistance. We didn't find anything outside that is suspicious, so we are finished here. Will you be available if we need anything?"

"Yes, you can reach me on my cell." Rhonda provided her number. As the officers walked away, Officer Matt turned around.

"Say, Rhonda, might you be able to get us a list of guests who stayed here this past weekend?" he asked.

"Well—Lillie takes care of all that business, but if I find some information, I will definitely let you know." She held up the card with contact information he had given her when they introduced themselves.

Rhonda returned to the crowd and offered to let them know if and when she had more information to report, and in the meantime, she excused herself and re-entered the inn.

Rhonda was as confused as anyone, but she went ahead with her work, beginning in the foyer. She was now far behind in her schedule, plus she wanted to visit Lillie at the hospital . . . assuming she was alive and would recover. She shook her head at the thought.

Rhonda did not get everything finished as she had hoped. She and Lillie always worked on cleaning together, but it was a lot of work for one person to complete in one day. By mid-afternoon she made herself stop so she could go to the hospital. Rhonda knew that

Lillie was an only child with a deceased mother, and she knew nothing about her father. To make matters even more difficult, she was unaware that Lillie had any close relationships.

Rhonda arrived at Norton Hospital late afternoon. When she walked into Lillie's room, she found her bandaged and asleep, so she sat with her for a bit, staring at her bruises, especially those on her face, which seemed to take the brunt of her fall. Occasionally Lillie would moan, which caused Rhonda to moan in sympathy.

A nurse came in to check her vitals. She was kind and gentle with Lillie, and she asked Rhonda if she was a family member.

"No. In fact, I don't know if she has any family. I work for Lillie, and to the best of my knowledge, she is all alone."

"That is sad to me," the nurse replied. "She sure could use some family love and support right now." She looked sympathetically at Lillie, then at Rhonda.

"Because of patient confidentiality, I'm not allowed to offer much information, but I hear her prognosis is good, although she is going to be hurting for a while," the nurse reported. "She is one lucky lady; I hear the fall was horrible."

"Indeed, it was," Rhonda responded. "I am the one who found her, and I thought she was dead. Thank you for sharing her prognosis with me."

Rhonda was grateful for the information, though she remained concerned for Lillie as she wondered who would help take care of her. Then she thought about scheduled guests and decided to return to the inn to see if she could find some information.

Maybe she has an insurance agent or an attorney, or perhaps she does have family, Rhonda thought. She gave Lillie a little kiss on her bruised forehead, and headed back to the inn.

Rhonda knew that Lillie conducted the business of her inn at the desk in her room, so that was the first place she looked when she returned. She had spent very little time in Lillie's room in the past. Lillie took care of the private quarters. She looked around the desk and hoped that the information she was seeking was not in the computer she could not access.

Lillie was neat and organized, skills necessary to manage a busy bed and breakfast, which she had done meticulously for years. Rhonda opened a couple of drawers and breathed a sigh of relief when she found an address book. She perused the book until she found the name of an attorney, and she took the chance this was someone who might help her. She dialed the number, but it was after the office had closed, and she had to leave a message. As she was returning the book to the drawer, she noticed several pictures of Lillie with some other folks. Rhonda thought she might find some information about relatives, so she viewed the snapshots, some of which appeared to have some age.

"Oh my God!" Rhonda exclaimed. "The dead man is Lillie's father!" She immediately called Officer Matt.

"Interesting," Officer Matt remarked. "Might you have a name or next of kin?"

"No, but if I find anything additional, I will let you know."

Rhonda was flabbergasted and exhausted. Both her physical body and her mind needed rest, so she returned home. On Tuesday morning Rhonda visited Lillie at the hospital again and was delighted to find her awake. Lillie was moaning and groaning and could barely manage a smile. Her face was bruised and swollen, and she looked like she had been hit by a truck, but she was just happy to be alive with no broken bones or serious damage.

Rhonda was somewhat reluctant to engage Lillie in conversation, realizing how difficult it must be for her, but she felt it was important to get some information.

"Lillie, I am so sorry for you. Do you know what happened?" Rhonda asked.

"Oh, yes," she replied, "I do," and she did the best to roll her eyes without causing herself more pain. "I just spoke to the police officers who were apparently at the inn the day I fell." It was hard for her to talk. She spoke with a soft voice, and enunciating some words was difficult due to her bruised and painful face.

"The man at my house was my father," Lillie explained, and Rhonda gasped.

"I didn't know he was still living," Rhonda confessed.

"Oh yes—he is—or was—quite alive until yesterday," Lillie explained. "I was to make arrangements to have him transferred to a nursing home or some type of assisted living facility this week."

"I'm so sorry, Lillie. I had no idea," Rhonda sympathetically replied. "What can I do to help you?"

"You have already been such a great friend, Rhonda. I'm so grateful that you arrived for work on Monday and called for help. I'm going to be fine. I think I'm better than I look, and as soon as I get off these pain killers, I will be able to think. I'm just so groggy."

"I understand, Lillie. Do you have guests arriving this week?" Rhonda asked.

"Yes, but only three. I try to take it easy the week after the fair, as there is usually so much work to do. The doctor said I should be released tomorrow morning. Might you be available to pick me up?"

"Of course, I would be happy to! In the meantime, can I call anyone for you or run any errands?"

"If you could pick me up in the morning, maybe we can talk about getting through the weekend. There is no one to call. My mother passed years ago, and I have no siblings, no husband and no kids. It must have been very confusing for you and the police, but I explained that Daddy was trying to come down the stairs by himself, and I reached for him when he stumbled. Then we both stumbled, and I didn't have the chance to catch my footing."

She failed to mention that she treated him for just one year the way he treated her for most of her life…hateful, with the exception of the physical abuse he imposed upon her. Lillie gazed off into the distance until she fell asleep, and Rhonda left.

Lillie's pain medication was reduced that evening, and by morning she was more awake. The doctor conducted his final exam of Lillie and discharged her by noon. Rhonda picked her up and delivered her to the inn by twelve-thirty.

Lillie was doing well at managing herself and was able to enter the inn on her own. Rhonda prepared them both lunch as they sat in the kitchen and discussed the upcoming schedule. With only three guests arriving on Friday, Lillie felt she could manage on her own, but Rhonda offered to finish cleaning the inn and stock the fridge, for which Lillie was grateful.

By the time guests arrived on Friday, Lillie was feeling much better. The bruises on her face still required some explanation to her guests, but Lillie saw no point in telling anyone the entire drama and simply explained an unfortunate tumble down the stairs was the cause.

Lillie arranged for her father to be cremated, with no pomp and circumstance. His ashes were stored in an urn provided by the crematory, and the urn was returned to Lillie, who eventually placed it in the basement where she didn't have to look at it.

Chapter 29

By the end of October Lillie had made a complete recovery. She was without bruises and pain. By November she was remodeling both the attic and room 3-B. Because the attic was equipped with a bathroom, she had plans drawn for a large two-story suite. The actual room was designed as a 'sitting room', and the attic became a large, king-sized bedroom. Windows were replaced by larger ones that invited more natural light. The bathroom was renovated, and the rest of the room was decorated in colors and fabrics that aligned well with the other rooms. The project was complete by the holidays, just in time for decorating.

While Lillie was busy with decorating, cooking, and maintaining the inn, she did so now with a great sense of relief and satisfaction. Her father was gone, and a burden had been lifted. No more secrets, no more guilt, and no more sneaking, she thought.

Lillie heard from Michael Roth that he would like to visit her during the holidays along with a photographer for an article he was preparing on the Lillie Inn Bed and Breakfast, and Lillie was happy to oblige. Michael said he would be bringing his fiancée, Maddie, and Lillie could not have been more delighted. When she hung up the phone she felt deep warmth in her heart, knowing that her inn was the meeting place for Michael and Maddie, maybe even a healing place for them both, and she loved the thought of being a part of their happy beginning.

Lillie began reminiscing about that great weekend in early fall and thought of Amy and Drew and the Little Baby Stout, hoping she would hear from them soon, as well.

Joan Jennings and Dr. Vic had reserved rooms for an upcoming weekend after the first of the year, another weekend Lillie would look forward to with happy anticipation as she realized that Joan and Dr. Vic's visit at the same time simply could not be a coincidence.

After healing from her tumble in October, Lillie returned a call to Sam, who left her a voicemail when she was in the hospital. Another happy reunion was being arranged.

Life was good for Lillie and getting better every day. She felt a happiness that was definitely worth the wait. She knew that as difficult as it had been, she now had peace and freedom that she likely would never have appreciated had it not been for the tough times. *Sometimes pain is the road to victory,* she thought, and she took a deep breath.

"One step," she said out loud, "one step at a time."

www.ingramcontent.com/pod-product-compliance
Lightning Source LLC
Chambersburg PA
CBHW031301170626
46807CB00001B/256